Jersey

Presents

CRYPT GNATS

Horror You've Been Itching to Read

An Anthology

Edited by Dina Leacock

JERSEY PINES INK

Welcome to Crypt Gnats

Cemeteries,

Graveyards,

Mausoleums,

Crematoriums.

Places for the dead so we can remember them.

Places that we treat with reverence and respect.

But these places can also attract.

They can attract a soul to its cremated form.

They can attract a need for revenge and to seek a Voodoo master.

They can attract self-proclaimed ghost hunters, unabashed thrill seekers, and curious grievers.

Like the phorid flies that are attracted to the odors of the dead, they are the crypt gnats, attracted to places of death for many reasons.

And if that reason is even partially selfish, they must be prepared to deal with the consequences.

Andrea Dawn, Tell-Tale Press

"Crypt-gnats dwells in the moments between life and death, that eternal grey world from which no travelers return. Or do they?

Here in these pages we journey to eldritch borders and see what some of the possible answers are. But, fair-warning Traveler, do not overstay your welcome.

There is an old Italian saying, *"Never reach out toward death or he will take your hand."* Some who you will meet here have disregarded such advice and enter the land of crypt and grave, seeking revenge, or answers to questions that should never be asked.

Some you will meet live in our daylit land and trade with the shadow world, taking both the wise and unwise to face it. Then there are the true monsters, who make the crypt and grave their home and exact a chilling cost from those who displease them.

Yet not all who travel its chill, dusk-haunted paths are evil, nor are they all damned. Maybe they just want to... well, live and let live...

So as you walk by the cemetery at night, do not stray, do not dare a short cut among the stone buildings and tilted monuments. Do not peer too closely at the shape that might have moved just at the edge of the light and disregard any entreaty or music you hear.

Hurry home, lock the door and retire to the fireplace with a good book, say this one...and maybe sleep with the lights on tonight."

Edward F. McKeown, author of *The Maauro Chronicles* and the *Robert Fenaday/Shasti Rainhell series*

Interior Design— River Cove Productions

Cover art — Dar Albert, Wicked Smart Designs

Additional editing — Andrea Dawn, Tell-Tale Press

Copyright © 2019 Jersey Pines Ink

ISBN 978-1948899-05-5

To the New Jersey Pine Barrens,
for giving me so much inspiration

CRYPT GNATS

Horror You've Been Itching to Read

Crypt Gnats Introduction

Well, after I titled this book "Crypt Gnats," to my utter surprise, I couldn't find crypt gnats in the dictionary, no wait, make that several dictionaries. *

I know they exist. I remember way back about fifteen years ago I was swimming with Beverly, the other half of Jersey Pines Ink, and she told me about them after she and her husband (he's a trustee on the board of a local cemetery) had attended a conference workshop on mausoleums. She mentioned crypt gnats and I recall thinking, what a cool name for a bug!

"I'm going to use crypt gnats in a story someday," I told her.

Fifteen years passed and I just never got around to writing a story about the nasty little creatures and all but forgot about it. When Jersey Pines decided we needed to put out an anthology, somehow we both remembered crypt gnats and decided it would be an excellent title for our first multi author book.

A little over a year after we came up with the idea for the book, *Crypt Gnats: Horror You've Been Itching to Read* is now published and ready to be read and enjoyed.

Editing the book was a fun, frustrating and fulfilling experience. In early 2019 I found myself retired for the second time and I spent the cold, dark, days of winter editing, and reediting and reediting. I never realized the amount of work that went into a book and my opinion of all editors out there went up dramatically.

There are twenty-nine stories of internment, cremation and creatures that lurk in graveyards. These tales take place in cemeteries, graveyards, mausoleums, and those special places where creative people have cleverly gotten rid of the body.

Released in the autumn, this book is perfect for reading during those late season hurricanes, early season blizzards and thunderstorms when those lights flicker and dim. Enjoy Crypt Gnats anytime you want because you won't be disappointed.

*FYI: When looking up crypt gnats I finally discovered that phorid flies are sometimes referred to as coffin flies, corpse flies and crypt gnats. In the larva stage they feed on decomposing bodies. Yum.

*This story reminds you that planning revenge
can be sweet, but be careful
of those lies.*

Gator's Magic

Tim Decker

It took rummaging through many freezing, hazardous back alleys to locate Gator and his rumored magic. But alley led to alley, tavern to tavern, back room to back room; what began as a simple *Know anyone who gives palm readings?* led to *Can you raise the dead?* I'd asked the first question of a bartender; I asked the last one of Gator. We'd been sitting across at a round table in the basement of a brothel located in a part of Baltimore where people not only carried weapons but kept them on display.

"I thought you wanted revenge," he said. His voice vibrated the marrow of my bones.

"I do. But the man I want revenge upon is dead."

"So you don't want revenge from me. You want resurrection." He slouched, but his eyes looked intent, as if they were drawing all his energy.

"Whatever you want to call it."

Without removing those eyes, Gator began drumming

the fingers of his left hand against the table. His long nails clattered; for a while, that was the only sound. Then: "This man . . . why not let him stay dead? Isn't that punishment enough?"

I still couldn't place his accent. His long face and tight, tan skin suggested the Mediterranean. People called him Gator because he was supposed to be from Louisiana.

"I need to kill him with my own hands."

"What did he do to you for you to desire such a thing, Mr. Mill?"

I cleared my throat and tried to look traumatized. "He killed my family—my wife and daughter. Harris was his name. Adam Harris. He broke into our house. Cut their throats. He tied me to a chair and made me watch."

I inwardly winced at the flimsy story, and at how the last several years had changed me.

Gator leaned back in his chair and looked me up and down for the hundredth time. "Why didn't he kill you?"

"He said he wanted to make me live with the memory. To suffer with it."

Gator finally looked away. I continued. "I recognized his voice when the police had me ID him. The Prosecutor still didn't think he had enough evidence. So I bought a gun, but then I read in the paper that the *former suspect*, as he was called, had died of a stroke."

Gator's profile seemed to contort: his lips pursed, curled upward in a half-grin, and then collapsed into a frown. "You must respect the magic. I cannot permit you to disrespect it. I've learned the hard way about its demands."

"I will always respect it." I spoke in what I thought was a solemn whisper.

2

His eyes, now looking sad, found mine. "I will do as you request, but we must meet again. Not here, but at my lodgings. One week from this moment." He spoke an address; I focused on committing it to memory. "Bring with you something meaningful. A picture. An heirloom. Someone's ashes." He rose abruptly and began moving towards the stairs.

"Wait!" I called out. He stopped but didn't turn around. "How much will you charge?"

Gator laughed, a slow, croupy chuckle, and continued on his way. I let myself out, moving past the women lounging in night gowns on moldy divans and torn recliners and chintz sofas that leaked foam the color of dirty cotton.

***

A week later, I searched for an hour during a constantly worsening snowstorm before I found Gator's address. The gang symbols changed—I was traveling far enough to venture into different territories. The houses grew larger and more dilapidated with increasing distances between them.

Eventually, I found a decayed Victorian with a porch and a balcony above it. The building seemed to lean forward, as if closely examining whatever appeared along the street.

A black kid answered the door, let me in and disappeared. The inside was so dark I found it difficult to imagine that light—even tepid grey light—existed beyond the walls. I reached under my jacket and felt for my Beretta slowly, as my eyes adjusted.

When a hand touched my shoulder, I flinched as if

stung by a wasp. Then Gator's tall body stood in front of me. "Do you like my home?" he asked.

"I suppose it's fine, if only I could see more of it."

We walked through a kitchen and descended a flight of stairs. In the basement, we came to a small room with cinder block walls and a card table. Some ancient-looking tomes were stacked on shelves in the back. The walls and floor were covered in odd drawings: satyrs discernible by their horns and grins and dancing hooves; shapes and symbols—mostly circles—that I'd never seen before; indecipherable runes.

Gator stood in front of me with his hand out. "Your item of importance, the one that is meaningful to you. Give it to me."

I stood to my full height and looked Gator in his eyes. "I don't have one."

His hand remained open between us, ready to accept.

"I found nothing of importance, nothing meaningful."

This much was the truth.

"So, no relic that reminds you of your wife or daughter?"

"Everything of theirs is tainted. I've gotten rid of it all."

I looked away and saw only his twisting shadow, darkly reproducing the protruding check bones, the pointed chin. He began to pace and shifted behind me.

I suddenly wanted to stop, surrender, go home and begin that which is harder than any revenge: the interminable process of accepting.

Then I felt agony radiating outwards from my pinky and upwards through my other fingers and penetrating up my arm, into my shoulder, down my side. I was released and fell face first upon a drawing of a snarling sun. I screamed and babbled.

Gator knelt by me and spoke incomprehensible words. A flame shot up from his index finger and he used the fire to cauterize my wound. Once done, he opened his other hand but I couldn't look at what he held. "I assume this was meaningful to you?"

***

I hadn't known we'd do the deed that night, but that's what Gator's timeline said, and he was the Taskmaster here. From a shelf, he snatched a small purple drawstring bag, and placed into it what he'd taken from me. He then stuffed the bag into a pocket in his black jeans and walked to the back of the room, returning with a bulky tome under his arm. "Now, it is time for us to do this wretched deed."

We took his rusted grey hatchback for a trip to Jessup Cemetery. The car had no windshield, and it snowed on us the entire way. The wind blew right in my face. I shook like I had malaria, but Gator didn't seem to be bothered.

With Gator somehow knowing where to go, it took us over forty minutes to reach the cemetery. As Gator pulled up alongside a black-iron gate, the sky grew darker. The gate opened smoothly and we walked without the assistance of paths, all of which had been covered by snow. Even with the presence of trees and headstones, I felt directionless and disoriented. Gator led the way.

Bare tree limbs, covered with coatings of snow, swayed and cracked; our footsteps squeaked beneath us on the accumulating layers. Tombstones seemed to expand upwards as the snow caked itself along their arches. Above our heads, branches from different trees entwined themselves within each other, forming a canopy made from the interlocking hands of giant skeletons. I thought about how peacefully Harris slept, embedded in his coffin.

I followed Gator's hunched shoulders past graves and flowers half-buried in snow. Then I heard chatter and clanking and saw two shapes emerging from behind a sprawling oak tree, heading our way. I swallowed cold air but couldn't breathe it back out.

I saw that it was two kids carrying shovels and pickaxes. One of them was the kid who'd let me into Gator's house.

"Why can't you use your magic for jobs like this?" said the one I'd never seen before. "That frozen ground is solid as rock."

"I've told you about respecting the magic," Gator said. "We can never use it for such petty concerns. It'll be easier when you throw the dirt back in. Return for that in an hour."

I saw them leaving us, becoming obscured by the snow and the trees, limbs reaching down from the claws of fleshless tricksters to tap the kids' shoulders.

Gator and I went in the direction they had come from, swerving around the oak. What followed happened only for a moment, but it remains one of the most surreal moments of that unnatural night.

The trees and gravestones and the black wrought-iron fence lined with spikes resembling arrowheads suddenly seemed like they could topple over. The snow, in fact, struck me as too dry, as talcum powder or sugar would look, and the dry leaves never crackled: they just fluttered

6

like paper. The patches of ground that featured uncovered grass resembled Astroturf. Overall, the cemetery looked *fake*, as if it had been constructed out of two-dimensional props. It smelled of plastic markers and Elmer's Glue.

Harris' grave was merely a rectangle in the ground. I didn't even see mounds of soil lying around it.

Then the piles of soil appeared, and the cemetery's wet snow and bitter wind and fluttering leaves returned.

"Why did you do that?"

"You have more pressing concerns now. There lies your friend."

We stood alongside the open grave; the coffin had already gathered a light coating of snow. Gator had been carrying his tome in the bag; he opened it to a page whose corner blew in the wind. He closed his eyes and whispered foreign words. I would've thought he spoke Latin, except the words had too many diphthongs. He held his left hand in the pocket where he'd placed the purple pouch.

I heard the coffin creak. When I first saw Harris' hands hoisting him from the grave, I thought they were pale leaves. When he stood upright, however, hunched forward, wearing the suit he'd been buried in, I wondered what Gator would do if I begged him to end this abomination. Amazingly, excitement stirred within me: I'd now die knowing that magic existed, but the sensation was short-lived.

Harris wore no expression. I saw few signs of decay on him—maybe a bluish tinge to the face—but I was afraid to look too closely.

I pointed my gun at Harris' head. I'd been aching for this moment. But that slouching beast wasn't him. Harris was dead. Stand his immobile corpse in front of me all day and night, and he'd still be dead. No sneer, no condescending glee in his eyes.

I lowered the pistol. "It's not him."

"I know." Gator looked at the sky, where the clouds passed by with unnatural speed. "You really wanted to kill this man, didn't you?"

"Yes."

Gator began advancing towards me. I noticed the corpse emitted no smell. "You see what I'm capable of, Mr. Mill. Now I'd like to hear the truth."

I looked at Harris, whose mouth had fallen open. "You already know it, don't you?"

"No, I do not. My magic has its limits. I only know that you lied."

I gave up. I could only beg, after all had ended, that he spare me the suffering he was capable of inflicting. "I've never had a wife or daughter."

Gator's face tightened; the wind stirred the corpse's hair.

"I do hate him. He made me that way, though. He was a sociopath. He convinced me that if he just had a person that everyone liked on his side in our department—a person like *me*—we could accomplish so much.

"Then, once I played the advocate and he got what he wanted, he started with the belittling." I detailed how Harris would call me his trusty sidekick, slap me condescendingly on the back, talk about his wife and kids and how I had neither, and made me look like a clown in front of people. I told how Harris slept with a colleague I'd been interested in and made sure I knew all about it. How he spread rumors to make sure no one else would hire me. I ranted and chronicled my slights.

8

"And now, even after he's dead, Mr. Harris has brought you here. He still controls you, doesn't he?" Gator walked around Harris and placed a hand on his tombstone. "Do you realize how seldom he thought of you?"

Gator then uttered some casual vowels. Harris lowered himself back into the ground, although I didn't hear the coffin lid close.

Gator removed the purple pouch and emptied it into the grave.

I wanted to run, but I suspected nobody could run from Gator. He muttered cryptically. A meatier hand than before appeared along the grave's edge. Then Harris stood before me and I saw how his body had grown compact, muscled, and about a foot taller. He held his half-clenched hands near his chest, as if preparing to reach out to grab my throat. Sinewy and stolid, he eyed me without menace, without recognition, but with a restrained power worse than any sneer or contemptuous smirk. This was a new Harris, refined by the magician for the occasion.

I shot him several times, but Harris only stumbled back a few feet before returning to his original position.

He reached out for me; even though I shot his hand, it kept reaching without bleeding. I knew there was no fighting him, so I ran.

While running, I heard Gator. "This is *your* Adam Harris, not mine, Mr. Mill. You created him." I tried not to listen, but his rich voice insisted. "He never started rumors about you; they existed because you're not good for much, are you? Your charming co-worker wanted him more than he wanted her. And now, revenge fantasies. You've been playing make-believe."

I somehow managed to keep ahead of Harris; maybe the snow made running difficult for his new legs, which were unused to this world's terrain. I remember his raspy, forced breathing, and I remember falling and expecting him to grab me as I scrambled for traction.

Somewhere, I dropped the pistol. I almost fell again when Harris unleashed a sound stuck between a squeal and a moan. I heard delight trying to screech through a broken throat. Eventually, I arrived at the wrought-iron fence and started climbing.

In my terror and haste, I placed my open hand down on a triangular spike at the top, putting my full weight on it—the same hand from which Gator had removed the pinky. When I felt the pain of the spike cutting into my hand, I pulled away with such force that I lost my balance.

I fell backwards, hoping that Harris would kill me fast. The fall knocked the wind out of me. As I lay in the snow, I saw Harris stomping towards me. Even in death, he remained superior.

It had stopped snowing and I shut my eyes, trying to drift as far away from reality as possible. I was shocked back into awareness by Gator's boot kicking me in the ribs. He assured me that Harris was gone and then reached down, scowling while holding out his hand. I offered him my good one. "The other," he said. I held out my injured hand and he took it, pulling me to my feet. By the time I was standing, the cut had healed.

I opened and closed the hand. "Why are you helping me?"

"What good would killing you now do? It would attenuate your punishment, and this time we speak of *my* style of punishing, not yours, which was simple-minded."

While listening to Gator, I almost wished Harris had ripped me apart.

He drew closer to me. "He will come to you. I might even join him; I despise those who disrespect the magic. Your suffering will be immense; your only taste of hope will be that it's not eternal. It may feel that way, however. Mr. Harris and I will see that you linger."

I last saw Gator leisurely meandering along while passing his bony claw across the tops of tombstones, pushing aside piles of snow that made brief, hollow thuds when they hit the ground.

Gator knew what he was doing. Every day, I wonder. What if Gator allows me to live the bulk of my life out, deciding to attack when I'm near death, a third-rate Faust awaiting a second-rate Hell? What if, on the other hand, Gator's promise of immense suffering comes my way tomorrow? In an hour?

Or never at all?

So I sit with a new pistol in my lap. I feel sure that if I raise the gun to my temple, Gator will be there with Harris in tow, and everything will be so much worse than if I just follow their timetable.

———◆———

Tim V. Decker grew up in Central Maryland and attended college at the University of Delaware. After spending a large chunk of the 2000s in Wilmington and Philadelphia, he moved North and currently teaches literature at Minnesota State University Moorhead in addition to writing fiction. His work will appear in Devil's Hour, an anthology from Hellbound

A story of having to let go.

Shadows and Bones

Art Lasky

The full moon is chill and heartless. Its bleak light leaches away all color; the bare tree limbs are tortured bones. Moon shadows dancing in the mist steal what little heat the stones once held. Shadows and bones, the cemetery: just shadows and bones.

I have memories of summer, but none of warmth. Winter coils within me. I feel cold, so cold. I bear it, knowing she will come. I drift. Time skips as I wait shivering among these shadows and bones. She must come.

She was a bookkeeper, I a salesman; neither of us the stuff of sonnets. There were few to note our union, and fewer to celebrate. Nonetheless we cared, one for the other, and our world was young and joyous. Two hearts blended in a Shakespearean flight of selfless passion. Until jealous fate decided that we flew too high, and let the heat of our joy hasten our fall into winter.

Suddenly, soundlessly, she is there in the swirling mist. Her face is drawn, yet her alabaster skin glows, a trick of the moonlight. She knows that I've been waiting; she smiles sadly and speaks.

"I'm sorry. But . . . but I'm here now. I miss you; I miss your smell, your touch. I miss the sound of you sleeping beside me, and the feel of our fingers entwined. Loneliness won't release its grip . . ."

There is pain in her voice; gone is the joy it once held. Gone too is the music and vitality that used to paint her words. Tears shimmer in her eyes, gelid splinters in the harsh lunar light. There is so much I want to say; I'm overwhelmed, speechless. I lean hungrily toward her warmth, she continues speaking,

"I love you too much. I can't let this anguish go on. For my sake . . . for our sake, let go. It's time to seek peace, to move on."

Reluctantly, I will let her go. I turn to leave, but something binds me to this place. Confusion. Slowly I remember: the doctors, the illness. The universe becoming a gray and narrow place, as a malignancy consumes my body. The pain barely diminished by powerful drugs. My body so weak, yet my mind so cruelly sharp. I watched her suffering in helpless sympathy. She remains with me until the darkness comes.

I let her go, and now there is nothing, just shadows and bones.

Art's a retired computer programmer. After forty years of writing in COBOL and Assembler, he decided to try writing in English; it's much harder than it looks. He lives in New York City with his wife/muse and regularly visiting grandkids.
Art's had flash fiction and very short stories published

Crypt Gnats

in Drunken Boat, Danse Macabre, Third Flat Iron, Fall Into Fantasy 2017, Neon Druid and Home Planet News Online. Please direct any comments, complaints, and demands for the return of the ten-minutes of your life you wasted reading his story to: ALASKY9679@YAHOO. COM

*Moving on can be hard and even harder
for some.*

Believing for a Reason

Diane Arrelle

Matilda Davis knew she was going to die. One minute she was driving too fast on an icy bridge and the next . . . well, the next was a series of images, crashing through the guardrail, the car landing on its roof with a bone snapping crack, and then the awareness of nothingness.

Puzzling feeling . . . nothingness.... "Am I dead?"

Laughter by many and a lone voice saying, "Give the woman a chance to acclimate."

"Hello?" Matilda called.

"Hello," a voice answered.

"Are you . . . are you God?"

The giggles started again.

"Cut it out," the voice called to the unseen crowd. Then to Matilda, "Do you want me to be your god?"

Matilda felt a wash of confusion. "My god? I . . . I don't have a personal god. Is this heaven . . . is this some sort of test to get in? Why are people laughing at me?"

Matilda was starting to feel emotions again and annoyance crept into her voice. "And what's with all this nothing? Why can't I see anything? Where are you people?"

The voice asked, "Do you have a god?"

"Hey, look, whoever you are. I don't have time for this mystical crap. Just answer my questions."

"Ah," the voice sighed. "An angry soul."

"The nothing will pass and, alas, it appears that you will have much time to contemplate the mystical crap, as you call it," a new voice said. "Anger is the first sign of the ones who do not believe. 'Tis sad, but—"

"What the hell?" Matilda yelled. "Stop talking to me like a bad eighteenth century novel. Just give me a hand and tell me how to get out of here."

Someone laughed.

"What is so goddamned funny?" Matilda snapped.

"You," the laughing voice said. "There are no hands, and no one here can tell you how to move on."

"True, true," the second voice said. "Thine own self is the only one, and if you do not know then, alas, you cannot know until you know how to know."

"Oh, quit talking like the Quaker Oats guy and just show me the way out!"

"Quaker Oats?" the voice said. "Of what does she speak?"

"It is the representative of a food company from our time, don't worry about it," the first voice explained. It then said to Matilda, "Look, newbie, I have my funeral to catch, so bye."

The second voice spoke again, "It is almost time. Do you not have any questions? I am a guide here to help the few who do not understand or believe. Open thy mind and see the ways."

"Why can't you talk like a normal person?" Matilda snapped. "How's that for a question?"

"A foolish one, but questions and answers are infinite here. Soon your mortal remains will be taken care of. Then you can pass on to whatever you believe, or you can remain."

This is just getting too weird, Matilda thought. *Why can't anyone give me a straight answer?*

Then suddenly, she could see. Naked bodies stretched out on steel tables and a huge yawning pit filled with flames, spewing out noxious gases and, for a second, panic gripped her. The Fires of Hell!

Then she realized where she was, that second-rate crematorium on the outskirts of town.

All around her, the dead babbled.

"Ooooh, look, that's me!"

"Wow, did I get smashed up or what!"

"My God, I'm green; I never looked good in green."

"Oh shut up!" Matilda screamed, wishing she had material hands to cover her ears.

"So who died and made you boss?" a woman giggled and was answered by peals of laughter.

The eighteenth century guide spoke up. "Anyone know not what to do?"

Everyone said they understood what they had to do, everyone except for Matilda and one other guy.

The guide said to both of them, "You can't move on until you have someplace to go. Do you not believe in anything?"

The guy said, "Yeah, I wanna go to heaven so I can drink beer all day long."

The guide asked in a puzzled tone, "Is that what you believe?"

The guy laughed. "Naw, but maybe I should, huh?"

Matilda groaned. "Come on, there is nothing to believe in. There is only me. I believe in me."

The guide had a resigned tone. "Then that is where you will be."

One by one, as the bodies were fed into the flames, the voices drifted away.

"I can't tell you what to believe, there is no right or wrong," the guide said, "only realize, you can't move on to another place if you don't accept that there really is another place. If you can't believe in anything, then you must remain tied to your earthly remains."

And the spirit guide was gone.

Real people moved around the three remaining bodies. "Yo, Harvey, it's almost five o'clock. Let's burn the last three together. The Jane Doe ain't going nowhere except in a box on the shelf over there with all the rest of the deadbeats. This guy don't got no family either so's he'll join her, and the smashed up bitch with the broken neck, well, her husband just said to do it cheap and put her in a cardboard box."

Matilda sniffed in indignation. "The nerve!" Then she watched in horror as they shoved her body into the flaming pit along with the two strangers. When the bodies were ash and bone fragments, the two men shoveled them into a box and sealed it with tape.

Suddenly Matilda found herself next to the other two

spirits. "Hey, it may not be much, but this is my box," she growled. "At least for now. This is some mistake; Gregory knows I wanted to be buried in a silk-lined casket. He knows I wanted a beautiful, ornate headstone. He knows what I wanted. He'll fix this!"

"Lady, shut up!" The man growled back at her. "Obviously your Gregory didn't give a shit what you wanted. You must have been one mean bitch to have him do this to you."

The girl that had been incinerated with them hummed. "You two must learn to get along," she finally said. "You both are going to be together a long, long time."

Then she was gone.

"Well at least the takes care of the crowding," the man said.

Matilda harrumphed and let her silence be her comment.

The next day or so, since time had no meaning in eternity, or so it seemed to Matilda, Gregory came and picked up the box. Matilda screamed, desperately trying to get him to hear her. "Greg, look what they've done to me. Fix this mess; get this guy and his damned ashes away from me. Greg, help me."

Gregory handed the man in the office some cash and carrying the sealed cardboard box like it contained a stinking, dead animal, went to the car, and threw it in the trunk.

Fear gripped Matilda for the first time. He threw her in the trunk! She saw all the empty fast food cartons and old newspapers and empty bottles surrounding her mortal remains and wondered if he would even be able to find the box in all this trash. And why hadn't she known about this secret stash of putridness? How could he have kept all this garbage a secret?

The car bumped along, then stopped and was turned off. She waited for Gregory to come get the box.

Nothing.

Eventually the car started again, and after time passed, it was turned off. This happened repeatedly. "I wonder why Greg hasn't had my funeral yet. Even if he can't undo the cremation, he could at least buy me a fitting urn and have my memorial service," Matilda mused as the car continued turning on and off.

"Hey, lady, you just don't get it. You're discarded. We are discarded. So why don't you shut up and let me spend my eternity in peace."

"Stop calling me lady. My name is Matilda."

"*Was* Matilda. Mine was Hank. Guess we ought to use our handles as long as we are doomed to spend forever together."

"Whatever," Matilda snapped and went back to waiting. "Just remember, this is my box, so back off."

Hank laughed. "I'll try, gladly I'll try, but Matilda, baby, it's kinda hard to keep my distance when our ashes are all mixed together like this."

"Look, you asshole, let's get the ground rules down. This is my box and you are just an awful mistake, just like you must have been in life."

Hank laughed. "Oh my, pot calling the kettle black time already? Why don't you just shut up, you stupid bitch, and think about your own life!"

Matilda did shut up. How had this happened to her, she

wondered. And why was she stuck forever with a stupid man she hadn't even known? She'd been a good person. She had watched over Greg making sure he didn't screw up too much. She'd taken care of herself, worked out every day and only ate healthy foods. She had spent their money wisely on the important things; she had done charity work to help the unfortunate wretches, she had even gone to church every Sunday even if she never got anything from it but gossip.

The car continued to start and stop, turn on and off. Occasionally the trunk would open briefly and another piece of fast food garbage would get tossed in on top of her remains. Hank had been silent, yet she felt his presence constantly. God, how she hated that intruder, and yet, sometimes the idea that she wasn't totally alone was comforting.

One day the trunk opened and her next door neighbor, Jillian, stood there holding the trunk lid with one hand, the other hand on her hip. She was frowning. Matilda snorted. "Look at that stupid cow, standing in those shorts, hand on her fat hip. That woman ought to have some pride and hide her heft in a sack."

Hank cut in. "I think she's pretty. And she's not fat, she's full."

"Shut up," Matilda snapped. "Mind your business. Jillian is *my* business. The fat cow is poking around in my husband's car, and this is my world, not yours."

"Thank God for that!" Hank muttered and went silent again.

Jillian turned around, smiled and yelled, "Greg, you're a pig! Bring me a trash bag, won't you, honey?"

"Honey?" Matilda sniffed. "Honey?"

Jillian grabbed handfuls of rubbish and started stuffing it into the bag Greg was holding. He was snuggling up to her, rubbing against her, nuzzling her neck. "Greg!" Jillian scolded. "This is disgusting! How could you keep all this stuff back here?"

Greg laughed. "Darling, this car used to be my only sanctuary from that obsessive bitch. I kept it a mess just to spite her. Childish, huh?"

"Well, I certainly can relate. She was . . . well . . . Matilda was bossy and a neat freak."

"Bossy? What a nice old-fashioned way to put it."

Matilda shrieked. "How dare they talk about me that way! How dare they."

Hank spoke up. "Well, they are, and they seem to be in agreement about you. Even I can see how awful you must have been and, we have no relationship at all."

Matilda ranted. "That's right, no relationship. You are an unwanted intruder, remember?"

Matilda stopped screaming long enough to watch Jillian and Greg kissing like teenagers and in front of her house. "That tramp!" she howled. "That slovenly pig has seduced my husband! I knew he was totally incompetent and unable to take care of himself. See, he hooked up with the first piece of fat ass that presented itself to him."

"I can bet you didn't have a fat ass!" Hank said. "Even having never seen you alive, I imagine that you worked out for hours every day and probably purged on the side. I can see you now: a leathery, sinewy, scarecrow with expensive clothes, lots of diamonds and a hard face covered in too much makeup. You were a clown, a caricature of what a human being was supposed to be. All I can say is good for Greg. He got lucky twice: once in finding her and once in losing you!"

Matilda started to answer, but was interrupted. Jillian had picked up the box. "Greg, what's this?"

"Trash," he said, "Just some trash I felt a need to hold onto."

"Oh . . . my . . . god," Jillian yelped dropping the box on the ground. "That's the crematorium's address and logo! Greg, you said you had taken care of Matilda!"

"Well, I . . . I . . . uh . . . I did. I kept her in the trunk where she's safe."

Jillian picked up the box. "Look, nobody liked her, but still, she was a person. Well sort of. Okay . . . ." she said as Greg stared at her and made a face. "Okay, but she was a human being and ought to be placed somewhere. Greg, she died last winter, before Christmas even, and next week will be Labor Day. That's just not right."

Greg looked down at the ground like a child caught doing something wrong. "Well, what do you want to do with her?"

"I'll buy an urn and we can keep her in the house somewhere. After all, it isn't like she's still with us or anything. It's just ashes."

"We . . . what does she mean we can keep her . . . that's my house . . . she can't be living in my house!" Matilda exploded. "And, oh God, no . . . she's going to buy my urn. I'm going to spend eternity in a blue light special! Tell me this isn't happening!"

Hank just laughed. "And I was afraid the afterlife was going to be boring!"

The box was brought inside, and Matilda saw how everything had been changed. Most of her collectables were gone, replaced with tasteless knick-knacks. The scattered pictures were of Jillian and Greg, and from the look of the hairstyles, the pictures spanned more than just a few months.

"That son of a bitch has been screwing her for years!" Matilda moaned. "He cheated on me and with a piece of low-class trash!"

Hank just kept on laughing.

Jillian placed the box on the top of the bookcase and went over to the computer. After a few minutes she called, "Hey, Greg, you won't believe the price we are getting for Matilda's china! I think we ought to buy her a great big fancy urn!"

Matilda felt faint. "My china! If I had a body, I'd just die!" she cried. "If I had my body, I'd choke her to death with all this dirt. Hasn't anyone dusted since I died? Oh Greg, I treated you so well, and this is how you repaid me?" A wave of melancholy washed over her. Everything she had done in life was being erased, everything she had cared about was being destroyed. "Oh, what have they done?"

Hank spoke up. "Maybe you should be asking what have *you* done? I know I wasted my life, and I'm trying to figure out how to stop wasting my death. Maybe you ought to be thinking about what we were told at the morgue. So many souls moved on, but we didn't. Doesn't that tell you something?"

"It tells me that I'm being unfairly and unjustly punished, otherwise why would I have you in my ashes?" Matilda snapped. "Go away and leave me alone. I obviously have more to worry about than your problems."

"Yeah, you do," Hank said in a soft tone. "I had hoped we could form a truce, form an alliance of some sort and figure out what they meant by believing, but I can see that being with you is an exercise in futility. I'll try not to bother with you anymore."

Day turned into night and back to day thousands of times, too many times for Matilda to keep track. The first time she had to watch Greg and Jillian make love, she screamed so much that Hank broke the short silence.

Now the silences were pretty well endless. They shared a box, but there was nothing to say. Hank once explained to her how he spent his time trying to understand why he was stuck in limbo. Matilda continued to fume and complain.

The house got worse and worse, filling with crap gathered from vacations and the very act of living. Matilda watched, unable to move as the box sat forgotten on top of the old dust covered bookcase. She watched Greg and Jillian age, wrinkle, and slowly wither.

She saw that death was going to come and claim them soon, and felt a grim satisfaction. She had never been able to forgive them for their happiness.

Boy, she mused as the hospice people left one evening. *I am finally going to give them a piece of my mind! Are they in for a surprise when they find out I've been here all these years!* Matilda felt happy for the first time in decades.

Hank spoke for the first time in years. "I sense you are happy, Matilda. That is good. I think you cannot move on until you learn peace."

"Oh God! Look who decided to butt in. I thought I was

rid of you. Well, for your information, I'm not happy . . . after all, you are still here."

Hank sighed. "My mistake. I though you were adjusting."

"Shit, if you're so adjusted now and understand so much, and God knows how an idiot like you could learn anything, then why are you still here?"

Hank sighed again. "I wish I knew. Someday I will." And he went silent again.

Sometime afterward, Greg was there, near them. "Oh!" he said. "Matilda!"

"Yeah, it's me, and I've been watching you with that slut in my house. How could you—"

"Matilda, good to see you," he said, interrupting her as if she hadn't spoken at all.

"Did you hear me?" she screamed at him.

"Why yes, sort of. Poor Jill, she will be sad. She doesn't fully understand that I am going to a better place. Oh, look, my body."

"Greg!"

"Matilda, why are you here? Oh my goodness, you are a ghost aren't you? Who is that?"

"Name's Hank. Our ashes got mixed together."

"Oh well, that is too bad. Look, a light!"

Matilda yelped. "What light? What are you talking about?" But she quickly realized she was talking to no one. Greg was gone.

"I saw the light!" Hank exclaimed. "I saw the guide! I think I understand. I understand Matilda! I believe! Hey wait for me!"

"Matilda," he shouted as if from a distance, "there is

more to believe in than yourself. Look inside you to look out!"

Hank was gone.

At first Matilda felt a surge of relief, and then fear. In all this time she hadn't had to face eternity alone.

"Hank?" She called, using his name for the first time. "Hank!"

The next day Jillian's children came and took her away. Time passed and Matilda stayed at her box, fully alone. Spiders spun their webs around her, laid their eggs, then eventually died. Matilda noted that even they moved on.

"What the fuck can a spider know that I don't? All right," she yelled. "I believe. Yep, I want to go to heaven. I'm ready."

Time continued to pass.

One day Jillian's children showed up and opened all the doors and windows. "Hey you guys," Matilda called although no one seemed to notice. "I'm up here!"

A woman suddenly looked up and frowned. "Hey, a box. A sealed box!"

"Treasure?" another slightly younger woman said.

The first woman ripped the tape that held the box closed, looked inside and screamed. "Oh, gross! It's full of ashes and some pieces of bone."

A man spoke up, "Yuck, look, it's from the crematorium . . . oh, disgusting. It has to be Hank's first wife. Oh, what was that bitch's name? Millie or something like that."

The woman dropped the box.

"Oh, look what you did! Now she's all over the floor," the younger woman said.

Matilda watched as the woman grabbed the broom and swept up her remains along with dust, dirt and dead bug carcasses. She dumped the pile from the dustpan back into the box, pushed the tape over the opening and threw it in a garbage bag.

"Oh no," Matilda shrieked. "What do you think you are doing?"

Time passed and then movement. The garbage bag was placed at the street and within minutes picked up by the trash truck. "Help!" Matilda screamed. "Help me!"

No one responded, but then, Matilda realized, no one ever did or ever would.

She continued screaming anyway as she was transported to the landfill. Garbage flowed out on top of the bag with the box, and Matilda realized that she was finally being buried.

She had an eternity of being part of the trash heap to try to figure out something to believe, but the only thing she could come up with was that life sucked, and death wasn't any better.

———

Diane Arrelle has had more than 250 short stories published as well as two short story collections: Just A Drop In The Cup and Seasons On The Dark Side. www.arrellewrites.com Facebook: Diane Arrelle

People can find solace in the strangest ways.

The Saint

Beverly T. Haaf

Patty's thoughts spun in a downward spiral in tune with the funeral dirge. *Down, down, down . . . around, around, around . . . gone, gone, gone . . .*

The pastor's voice rose above the dying notes of the organ as he spoke the name that had gathered Patty together with fellow mourners. "Fredrick Ralston Paine," the pastor said in ringing tones. "Fred Paine: a good man, a man we all knew and loved."

"Amen," said someone, and more *amens* echoed in a murmured drone.

"Beloved Fred," said the pastor, lifting his arms as if to heaven.

Patty lifted her gaze to the urn on the cloth-covered table in front of the altar.

Beloved, she thought, her lips barely moving as she whispered his dear name.

The woman beside her placed a gentle hand on Patty's arm. Patty leaned toward her, seeking comfort even while knowing the comfort that had been hers would never be hers again.

Since Fred's death Patty had heard repeated stories of his dedication to the church, his generosity to community efforts and of his reputation as a businessman who truly cared for those he served. His printing company had continued to flourish despite on-line options thanks to Fred's charm and his personal touch—banners, signs, business cards, flyers, fundraising letters, anything that customers needed that could be printed. Fred's caring and attention to detail made the difference. Especially to his church where he was so dearly beloved, for there was never a charge.

"His generosity was his gift to God," said many, and others said, "He was God's gift to us."

"So even-tempered," a neighbor said. "He never raised his voice, never became angry."

"Only twice," Patty said, "and then with good reason."

"Even a saint has his moments," the neighbor had soothed.

Many told Patty how they would miss seeing Fred walking with her and his yellow Labrador retriever, Toby.

"Patty," the pastor had said, "I hope you don't blame Toby."

She thought of Toby, a soft butterscotch color, small for his breed and so sweet-tempered. "No," she had said, "that wouldn't make sense."

Everyone knew what had happened. Fred and Patty had been walking the dog with Fred greeting everyone along the way. Children ran to fuss over Toby while Fred stood by proudly. But after they moved past the houses to the meadow path, Toby, off leash as was customary in that area, bounded after a squirrel, tripped, fell into a ditch and was knocked out. Fred had lifted the unresponsive animal from the ditch and dashed back for the car, but after an emergency ride to the veterinary clinic, the sad news was that Toby had to be put down. Then, on top of that shock, came a shock even more horrifying: grief-stricken Fred dropped dead from a heart attack in the clinic parking lot.

The double loss left Patty churning in confusion, not only from grief, but also from the strain of trying to get everything done at once because she couldn't bear to draw it out.

Quickly, she arranged for the grave's monument stone. Fred's church allowed cremation, but interment in the ground was necessary—ashes to ashes, dust to dust— even though the ashes were contained in an urn. Tears flowing, Patty ordered the stone to read *FREDERICK RALSTON PAINE,* the birth and death dates and then—a special inscription.

The funeral service came to a close. Before handing the urn to the funeral director for internment, Patty kissed it and pressed it to her cheek. *So cool to the touch,* she thought, again allowing her tears to flow, *so unlike the comforting warmth of life.*

At the reception after the funeral, fellow mourners repeated their sympathies and praise-filled memories, but at last Patty was free to return to her lonely house.

There, still teary-eyed, she remembered her life with Fred.

All the things people believed about him was correct when he was outside the home, but inside it, he was the opposite: impatient, controlling and cruel, with a temper that erupted over Patty's every flaw, from a wrinkle in an ironed shirt to a speck of dust, to food not to his taste and then dashed to the floor.

Patty, a stranger to the town, had entered the marriage bringing Toby with her, but Fred so enjoyed the image of a man and his dog that he allowed people to believe Toby was his. Patty, having learned that Fred wasn't the man she thought she'd married, knew to say nothing. On that fateful day, once they were away from those who knew only his public face, he flew into a rage over some imagined fault, a rage so volatile that mild Toby growled. Fred's fury flashed to the dog and he slammed Toby between the eyes with the edge of his cell phone.

Toby collapsed and despite Fred's kicking the animal's ribs, Toby only moaned. Cursing, Fred left Patty sobbing over Toby, and returned with the car to take the dog to the vet. Patty knew he couldn't have anyone thinking he didn't treat *his* dog right. He grabbed Toby by the scruff of his neck and started dragging him over rough ground toward the car. Toby, showing his temper for the second time, snarled and tried to twist around as if to bite. Fred kicked Toby in the head.

In the vet's office, after Toby was put down, Fred appeared heartbroken as he settled the bill, but in the deserted parking lot, he erupted in an arm-flinging rage over the cost for the "idiot dog." In the midst of his fury, he suddenly gasped and dropped dead.

With Fred's body at her feet, Patty knew what she would do.

When the ashes arrived from the respective crematoriums, she emptied Fred's ashes from the beautiful urn she'd ordered and replaced them with Toby's ashes, which had come in a cardboard box.

All Patty's tears at the funeral were for Toby. The headstone might bear Fred's name, but it was Toby who would rest under it, and the inscription on the stone would be all for Toby, *THE TRUE SAINT*.

Fred's ashes?

Patty liked to remember how she had ground them down the kitchen garbage disposal.

Down, down, down . . .

Around, around, around . . .

Gone . . . gone . . .

Gone.

———

Beverly T. Haaf is the author of six novels. Her short fiction has appeared in numerous magazines, including Ellery Queen and the anthologies, Book of the Werewolf and Crafty Cat Crimes. She is also editor and publisher of a monthly newspaper for four municipalities and co-publisher of Jersey Pines Ink, LLC.

*A tale that warns to not disturb the
sleeping dead.*

Bonedigger

John Higgins

On an August night in the remote town of Conner's
Mill, everything was about to come undone. It was 1979; I
was eleven years old, disco was nearly dead, and I was already looking forward to next summer, when *The Empire
Strikes Back* would come to theaters.

My bedroom window was open and the gentle, humid
breeze hissing through the trees had lulled me into a thick
sleep. A sudden sound jarred me awake, a dull thrum that
set my hair on end and filled me with panic. Pictures rattled against the wall. The Star Wars figures on my shelf
scooted around randomly, like my cousin's tabletop vibrating football game.

I ran to the window and saw bedroom lights coming on in the neighboring houses. People leaned out of
windows, and others walked out into the night. They all
looked hesitant, terrified.

Beyond the clutch of houses lining Main Street were
side streets stitching a half-mile into the outlying rural

land filled with what had once been farms, now overgrown and forgotten.

The low droning persisted, rattling my back teeth.

Mom, Dad, and Dave scrambled down the stairs and loudly exited the front door of the house, chattering all the way about what the hell was going on. I rushed out to join them. Dave, my brother who was four years older, was the only one who took notice when I appeared behind them though the open doorway. "Hey," he said, distracted, looking alternatively up at the night and then to the horizon.

I nodded at him.

The sky above was streaked with an eerie, dull, gray light that seemed to be coming from behind our house.

Mom and Dad, in their nightclothes, tentatively walked off the porch to the concrete walkway in front. Dave darted through the house and out the back door, toward the source of the light. I was a few steps behind him. I could hear Mom and Dad calling to us, telling us to be careful.

What we saw in the backyard stopped us cold. About fifty yards away, a yellow glow seeped through the tree line and down the hill toward us. The acrid smell of burnt hair was on the breeze. We knew what was back there, over that hill.

"The old cemetery," Dave said.

We had discovered it last summer and had treated it like our little secret, but everyone knew about the scattering of headstones back there. Dad said it just was a private plot for some farming family long ago. The farmhouse had burned down sometime in the last century, and the forest had since overgrown all that land. The headstones were faded; most had no dates, only names—old-time names like "Jeremiah" and "Esther." No one went back there, and Dad told us never to go there again.

We went, though. Every time we walked back in the woods for an adventure, we'd end up there and look around at the headstones laid out seemingly at random. We told ourselves how cool it was to wander over the buried bodies of people long dead, but mostly we secretly went there because Dad told us not to.

The last time we were there, just yesterday, I saw someone: a tall man, dark, cast in shadow, peering at us from behind a tree. I stopped and stared at the dark shape, deciding if it might be a trick of the light. Dave had looked where I pointed but said he didn't see anything. I figured it was my imagination; it was just a shadow between trees at twilight. I didn't want to push my luck and give my brother another reason to call me a wuss, so I just fell quiet and ignored the shadow as best I could and stuck close to Dave.

After we came back, I didn't say a word about it, but I couldn't shake the feeling I was being watched.

Now, the low thrum and yellow glow was coming from that cemetery on the ridge.

"Oh, no," Dad said as he approached from the back door. He and Mom walked right past us, eyes fixed on the sickly yellow shine.

"That's the bell," I heard Mom say under her breath. She shot a sidelong glance at my father. "It has to be."

Dad shook his head. "Can't be."

About twenty people from nearby houses filtered into our backyard, transfixed by the glow. I looked at them; all were agog and gaping . . . all except Old Man Landon, who lived three doors down and was known to be as mean as a wolverine. Everyone let him be, especially the neighborhood kids. Mom said he wasn't always so foul, but had some bad things happen to his family that she would rather not tell me.

I tried to keep that in mind, that maybe he was just a sad old man, in spite of the fact that he kept a rock-salt gun near his front door to shoot any kids who cut through his yard—at least that was the rumor.

He caught my eye and stared. "Did you go up there, Jason Grant?" He had greased-back white hair, a beer gut barely contained in his bathrobe, and wild, blue eyes, one slightly larger than the other. The effect of his eyes was exaggerated when he was angry; one bulged and the other receded into his skull just enough to be both funny and creepy.

In a terrifying moment I will never forget, the gaze of the neighbors around him uniformly turned toward me in a silent, accusatory stare.

"What?" Dad said suddenly and moved closer to me. "Of course he didn't."

Mr. Landon came toward us with his pronounced limp that made him seem even more menacing. "It's on your property, and we know your boys have been up there."

"That was last year," Dad said, maybe not strongly enough to sound confident. "I told them not to go there again."

"They been there," a woman's voice called out from the other side of the house. "*I seen 'em!*"

The voice was distorted by the low thrum, so I didn't recognize it. Maybe it was Mrs. McGrath, our next-door neighbor who was too concerned about the state of our lawn and whether we shovel the sidewalk free of snow in a timely manner.

"Did you boys go up there, since that first time?" Dad said softly under his breath. Mom looked down at us, brown eyes wide and panicked.

"A few more times," Dave said quickly and moved closer to me, either to guard me or throw me in front of Dad's wrath. "It didn't seem like a big deal."

"Did you see anyone up there?" Mom said a little too loudly. Old Man Landon caught onto that and took a few steps closer to us, so he was now a little more than ten feet away.

"It saw your boys," Mr. Landon said to my father. "There ain't no doubt. They made it hungry again." He pointed at the glow. "That sound is his bell, built from bones and souls. Bones of the people it takes." His voice rose in pitch. "I heard it before. It rings from the other place. From *his* place. It calls us."

His voice rose like a big-top preacher calling for sinners. His course, strident words woven into the thick current of the bone-shaking tone sent a chill from my legs straight up to the base of my skull. "Something made it take notice. Something made it hungry. *Someone* brought it back," he said, pointing at me and my brother.

A gasp rippled through the crowd. Most of them began backing away from us; a few stumbled and others ran home.

The deep thrum shifted lower, like another bell being struck. The sound became a vibrating presence in my chest, seeming to grab my heart and break its rhythm into fits and starts. All the lighted windows, streetlights, and doorways went dark. We were illuminated only by the glow from the woods and the stars peering down indifferently from a moonless sky.

"The earth wants tribute. A tithe," Mr. Landon shouted. He turned to the remaining people slinking into the shadows behind him. "If you're old enough, you heard the stories about it."

Cars up and down the street began to grind and whine as drivers cranked their engines. Not one of them started, as if all the energy in the town had been devoured.

"Goddamn you, Tom," Mr. Landon hissed at my father. "Goddamn you for not telling them."

"It's *bullshit*," my father barked at him suddenly. His pitch rose with fear. "Who would believe something like that? The Bonedigger. The earth up there eats cadavers. Jesus Christ. It's a kid's story."

"*Does that look like a goddamn kid's story*?" Mr. Landon was spitting as he shouted; his voice quivered. He took a breath and turned to the shifting crowd behind him. "Maybe we'll give these two," he pointed at me and Dave. "It got their scent. It got their taste."

A murmur spread through the dozen panicked humans who still remained in our yard. "Yeah," someone said. "Maybe," I heard another say. "What do we have to lose?" said another, verging on tears. It was too dark to clearly see faces, but I didn't need to. These people were no longer the people I had known before the sound had come. They were not neighbors. They were a terrified mob.

The deep tone filling the air had a maddening effect. I could feel panic slipping into my thoughts. It was there in everyone's eyes, too. It became hard to think about anything but fear.

Mr. Landon bent down and picked up a fist-sized rock. "It's what we have to do, Tom."

Some in the crowd followed suit, picking up rocks. Others were motionless, watching. Dad stood in front of me and Dave. Mom screamed at them to put down the rocks.

Amid the panic, I felt something new enter my mind. Something moved through my thoughts, sniffing in the dark . . . hunting.

"I see him!" a woman's voice called. "*I see him!*"

All eyes scanned the tree line, including mine. There was a gap in the glow between the trees. A shadow blocked the shine; it was vaguely in the form of a man, like the thing I'd seen in the cemetery. It didn't move toward us; it just seemed to grow larger and arced across the sky, snuffing out the stars.

Screams of panic shimmered through the crowd.

Dad leaned in close. "Root cellar, now," he growled.

Dave grabbed my arm and we sprinted around the people to get to the back door. I swear I heard them on our heels, screaming. I even think I heard a rock hit the wall as we ran inside . . . but that could have just been the pounding of my heart.

We crossed the kitchen and thundered down the basement stairs. Dave pulled the door shut. The sickly yellow glow from the woods cast just enough of a pall through the basement's dirty rectangular windows for us to navigate the dark, musty cellar.

I could hear the screams of panic become serrated

shouts of rage. Dad yelled from the yard, telling them to stop, to think, to back off, to get the hell out of his house.

The thing slithering through my mind wrapped around my thoughts and showed me what it would be like to grab my brother by the neck and start tearing into his body, pulling him apart one handful at a time and leaving his flesh for the worms. I stopped, stunned at this vivid vision.

Dave screamed my name and squeezed my hand hard enough to nearly crush the bones. The pain caused the dark image to crumble away.

"Come on!" He raced toward the far side of the basement with me in tow.

The root cellar was a small sub-basement built over a hundred years ago. Two concrete steps led down to a small wooden door no more than four feet high. We didn't use the root cellar for anything; it was little more than a curiosity in this old farmhouse but had once served as cool storage for a time before refrigerators became a household staple.

That tiny room was unlit, damn cold, filled with the smell of earth, and utterly terrifying. It was like a grave.

Dave didn't hesitate to drag me in there. I was immediately assaulted by spider webs; gossamer tendrils clung to me. Gunfire cracked from above. People scuffled on the hardwood floors. We heard thumps, screams, and then the noise moved into the streets. Shouts and raging words filled the night, but no one came down into the basement.

"We have to help Mom and Dad," I said. My voice was shaking and weak. My stomach turned and my body was stiff with fear.

"We can't do anything," Dave's voice was flagging; he was trying to keep the sadness and shock from his words.

"I can get to the kitchen. *I can call the cops!*"

"No, don't. Dad told me about this."

"About what?"

"Bonedigger. He said it was a bullshit local legend. It was something the farmers around here used to worship or make sacrifices to. That's why they put the graveyard there. It was like an offering. But Dad said it was just a . . . a . . .," his voice broke. In the darkness, I could imagine his face twisting with pain. "It was a story told to keep kids off those farmlands back there. Just a story."

I reached out to comfort him, but as I touched his bare arm, the thing in my thoughts showed me again how perfect it would be to tear my brother apart. The blood would be succulent, the flesh sweet. The shadow, the Bonedigger, wanted to chew him to a crunchy pulp.

I closed my eyes and moaned, pushing down those images.

To this day, I never told him those terrible thoughts that had invaded my mind that night. I wonder if he's also keeping the same secret from me. Maybe it wasn't only sadness tearing at his voice.

The low peal of the bell stopped, leaving only distant screams from above. As the low tone faded away, so did the thing invading my thoughts. The horrible images ceased.

Unseen tiny creatures tickled across my skin as I sat on the earthen floor, frozen in utter blackness for hours, unable to move. We waited until the world fell silent.

Dave and I emerged from the root cellar, stiff and cold. Daylight streamed through the two small, squat rectangular windows that faced the street in front of our house. Dave tried to peer through, but the glass was too clouded with age and filth to see clearly what lay beyond.

We crept up the creaky staircase and opened the door. It was awful, a nightmare. Blood coated the kitchen floor. It was as slick as fresh oil on the ceramic tiles. Cringing, we stuck together, arm in arm to gingerly control our footing. Eventually, slowly, we examined the entire house, calling for our parents.

"Maybe they're in the woods. Maybe they got away," I said to Dave with desperation in my voice.

"Yeah, maybe," Dave said. I saw his jaw clench under his skin.

Blood had soaked into the carpeting of the living room and slicked the walls and staircase leading to the second floor. Upstairs, two of the three bedroom doors had been broken down. My room had blood on the walls in great splashes and arcs. I felt violently sick to my stomach and fell to my knees.

Dave helped me up. "C'mon. Let's get out of here," he said.

Outside, it was the same—blood, no bodies.

We shouted for Mom and Dad until our throats were raw. We went into other houses and ran up and down the street. At one point, I sat down on someone's lawn and cried until my stomach ached and I could barely draw a breath. Dave hugged me close, like Mom used to do when we needed it.

He sobbed quietly. "We'll be okay, buddy," he said. The unexpected affection from the brother who usually took delight in tormenting me made me gather myself faster than I thought possible. I drew a deep breath and nodded.

"We'll be okay, buddy," he repeated, mostly to convince himself.

Some stragglers, like us, came out into the bright day and blue sky. All were haggard, stunned, silent.

Only one hundred and twelve people of the four hundred residents of Conner's Mill lived through that night. The days following that morning became a dull blur in my mind. We spent time at a hospital, then our legal guardian, Aunt Laurie, came up from Philadelphia and took us in.

I never returned to Conner's Mill.

Over the next four decades, a host of paranormal and unsolved mystery reality shows went to that little town to do a story about the Legend of Bonedigger—usually around Halloween and usually with cheesy special effects and cheesier actors. Conner's Mill and the Bonedigger even have their own Wikipedia page.

And throughout the years, investigators have repeatedly searched for clues. No corpses were ever found. Not a single bone, tooth, or hair. Everyone just vanished on that night, like the earth had swallowed them whole.

And somehow I just know that the Bonedigger slumbers by his graveyard. At peace, at least for the time being.

———

John Higgins lives in northeastern Pennsylvania, has a Bachelor's degree in English and computer programming, and currently is employed as a network engineer. He has wonderful twin girls who share his love of reading. He has a published horror novel, Soulscape. "Bonedigger" is his first published short story.

A story that shows life will find a way.

Born in a Casket

Ben Fitts

My mother was cold when I was born. Much colder than I am, and I am not exactly burning to the touch. You could maybe describe me as lukewarm, somewhere between the two extremes.

During my birth, I ended up having to squeeze myself out of her unassisted, because there was no one around to help me. It was a challenge at first, but her flesh was soft and loose and had a lot of give to it and I found my way out eventually. It was very dark when I was born, but thin rays of pale light bled in from a crack in the ceiling, and soon enough my eyes adjusted to it.

After I finished emerging from her womb, I crawled up the length of her body to look my mother in the face. She had carried me inside her for my whole life up to that point, all nine months of it, and I was excited to finally meet her properly. I had never heard her speak during the entirety of her pregnancy with me, although I had heard my father speak during his infrequent visits. I was eager to meet him as well and was somewhat disappointed that he had missed my birth. It was an important milestone if there ever was one.

"Hello, Mother. Have you decided on a name for me yet?" I inquired once I reached her face. I was still a new-born and very small back then, and I was able to comfortably cradle myself on her exposed collarbone while I spoke to her. My mother did not answer me.

I tried to look into her eyes to see if there was some emotion hiding in them that may provide some sort of explanation for her silence. As I looked, I was surprised to see nothing more than a pair of empty sockets returning my own puzzled gaze. I examined her face more closely then.

She had more bone than skin showing, although strips of grey flesh still clung to her skull in places. Her nose was similarly absent, with again nothing but an empty socket where it should have been. Her lips were gone as well, and she had no choice but to perpetually grin a toothy smile. Her head was framed by long strands of brittle grayish hair.

A chain necklace hung from her neck, from which hung a flat triangular pendant made of fine silver. Although it had become rather dusty, it was still clearly a thing of beauty and I eventually came to spend hours staring into it.

I found myself wondering if I might resemble my mother. I wondered if I too had bones showing and rotting skin and missing parts. Sadly, I had no mirror to look upon myself back then so I was forced to discover this information the best I could through other methods. I looked down upon my own naked body, examining my own thin forearms and belly, my legs and tiny genitals. My skin was a similar drab shade of grey as hers, although mine had some traces of pinkness that hers was devoid of. Also, I did not have any bones showing.

I grabbed a handful of flesh from my greyish thigh. It felt soft and unripe. As I tugged on it, I found that it was easily stripped away. I clawed at it, tearing away of a chunk of it until there was nothing but shiny white bone. I decided then that I had better cease ripping away my own flesh, in case I decided I wanted it back later. I instantly regretted the bit of my thigh that I had torn off, but we can all be rather foolish in youth.

I stroked my face with my hand, feeling its curves and appendages. Unlike my mother, I certainly had eyes, big squishy round things, a nose and lips. I wondered if some of these differing traits were ones that I had inherited from my father. I was desperate to meet him and see for myself, and I wished so that he would come visit sometime soon.

I found myself growing tired then. My first day outside of the womb had been exciting, but also rather exhausting. I curled myself into a comfortable position and slept.

After that first day, my life fell into somewhat of a predictable pattern. I would wake and tell my mother good morning, although she never responded. I often tried to speak of other things to her throughout my waking periods, but she was resolute in her stillness. I wondered if she had taken a religious vow of silence, if she was perhaps a devout Buddhist or Hindu. There was so much that I had left to learn about her back then. Then, once I felt my weariness grow again, I would curl back up and fall asleep once more.

This routine occurred without variation for some time. I noticed myself growing rapidly. My body was squished closer against the velvet-lined walls of our home as there became less and less room for both my mother and me. I took this as a sign that I was growing up, and soon it would be time to finally leave the proverbial nest. I wished that I would get a chance to meet my father before I left, that my childhood would not be just another spent without a paternal figure.

I tried pushing the roof off our home. I jammed what I could of my slender fingers under the thin opening where our light trickled in order to gain better leverage as I pushed. But no matter what I did, I could not get the thing to budge. I was simply not strong enough, which in retrospect was to be imagined, as I was still only an infant then.

One day, I decided to try and push the top of our home and climb out one last time. If I again failed to accomplish this task, I would take it as an indication that it was not in fact time yet to leave home, and that I would be strong enough to make my exit when I was truly ready to.

Unsurprisingly, I failed once more. But, I did manage to come closer than ever before, as while I did not entirely liberate our home from its roof, I did manage to push it up just ever so slightly. This was something I had never accomplished in any of my previous attempts. As I fell back to the ground, drained from the effort, a good deal more light from the now wider opening spilled into our home than previously ever had.

I was blinded at first. It was more brightness than I had ever been exposed to in my life, brief as it still was then, and it was enough to greatly disorient me. After I recovered and adjusted to the new lighting conditions in our home, I gasped.

The light struck my mother's silver pendant directly, making the pale metal glow. I squirmed over to the necklace with hope bubbling inside me. I licked my thumb and wiped away the dust and grime that coated it and giggled in sheer delight at what I saw in the new light.

My own face gazed back at me from the pendant's triangular surface. So this is what I looked like! I arched an eyebrow and stuck out my tongue. I laughed gleefully when I saw my reflection mimic my exact movements. I had the same sharp chin as my mother, and I also had her high, pointy cheekbones. I spotted the little wisp of hair that I had recently felt growing upon my scalp. It was black as a raven's wing. There was no way to know if I had the same eyes, nose or lips as my mother, but if I ever met my father I would likely be able to tell by means of deduction.

Staring at my reflection in that triangular pendant became a joyous and eagerly anticipated part of my routine each day. I would still say good morning to my mother each time I woke and attempted to engage her in conversation in the hopes that this would be the day she finally spoke. But no matter what I tried to speak to her about, whether it was questions about my father, my recent discovery of the pendant's reflectiveness or the poetry of William Blake, I could never find a topic captivating enough to animate her. Then I would stare at my reflection, making different faces and mimicking expressions in front of the pendant hanging around her neck until I felt the need to return to sleep. It still amazes me how small my world once was.

Crypt Gnats

On one such day, as I was viewing myself in the pendant's reflection, I heard heavy footsteps from outside our home. I had been looping my index fingers into either side of mouth and pulling my lips apart from each other, revealing my rows of brown teeth and blackened gums. I removed my fingers from my mouth and spun onto my back, propping myself up on my elbows. While light spilled in through the crack in our home, there was nothing to see by looking out of the crack other than blackness and distant spark of blinding light. This meant that I was unable to peer out and see whom approached.

My heart quickened with excitement as I heard the footsteps draw nearer our home. They stopped directly outside.

"Ya miss me, baby?" I heard a deep, raspy man's voice say.

"I trust you've been good while I've been away. No trips to Paris with my credit card or anything," he said, chuckling to himself.

Suddenly the top of our home was being lifted upwards, a light poured in from above. I blinked, and then stared up at the man standing above us. He was bald, with a patchy red beard. He wore a green polo shirt, flip flops and dirty sweatpants that he had lowered so they sagged around his ankles. He had the same hooked nose, the same hazel eyes as me. And that voice! How had I not recognized it instantly? It was the other only voice I had ever heard aloud, other than my own.

"Father!" I cried, looking directly up at him. "I am delighted to finally make your acquaintance. Tell me, have you and Mother finally decided upon a name for me?"

Crypt Gnats

My father's eyes widened as he saw me. He then shrieked. It remains to this day the shrillest, most piercing noise I have ever heard. He turned around and sprinted away, tripping over the sweatpants that he had forgotten to pull up. He scurried onto his back, hoisted his pants back up and bolted up a flight of stairs and out of sight, leaving the roof of our home open.

"Father, where are you going?" I called after him as I stood up. It was the first time I had ever stood fully on my own legs, and they wobbled underneath me. I had to grab a wall for support. Peering over the side of the wall, I studied my surroundings.

Our home was on top of a black marble floor and encased by smooth granite walls with stained glass windows. The staircase on which my father had fled was against the far wall and led to a thick stone doorway. Etched onto the granite wall, directly above my home, were the words:

MARY ELIZABETH BARNES

1987-2009

SEVENTH DAUGHTER AND LOVING FRIEND

Below the inscription, there were further etchings of symbols whose significance eludes me.

I had been standing for a while by then and was feeling more confident about walking on my own legs. I hoisted myself up and out of the casket where I had lived my whole life and walked through the mausoleum and up the steps. I could not reach the handle on the door, but my father had left it just slightly ajar as he fled. I squeezed my thin, infantile body through the crack and finally walked out into the world.

———•———

Ben Fitts is a writer, musician and zinester from New York. He is the author of over twenty published short stories and the creator of the zines The Rock N' Roll Horror Zine, A Beginner's Guide To Bizarro Fiction and Choose Your Own Death. He has played in the bands Spastic Fitts and Ash Chugger and makes witchy solo music under the name Capra Coven. He's had stories published in Horror Sleaze Trash, Weird Mask and F•cked Up Stories To Read In The Daylight

Burial can happen in different ways.

Denizen

Mike Rader

In the tomb of the sewer he reigned supreme, a crawling figure, traversing the slimy bricks on all fours, his bright eyes keen and alert to any danger. No rat dared draw near. No reptile, no creature challenged him.

He had not seen the surface for two decades, not since he was brutally attacked by his own men and thrown down an open grating. Where was their respect? Hadn't they sworn an oath of loyalty? But they'd left him for dead. His younger brother had been one of them. He'd shouted down after him: "They'll never find your body."

His clothes had rotted long ago. Now he was clad only in rough sacks that he had found in the mire.

Every so often he was aware of the presence of other humans. Workmen. Inspectors. Their flashlights probed the old tunnels and drains. Their voices called to one another. And then they would go and leave him to his world.

He ate whatever he could find. Rats, birds, bats, his stomach long ago accustomed to flesh of every convenient kind.

He knew he had a name. It was Matteo. Teo for short. He knew he had once been a powerful man, controlling an empire of vice and drugs. Sometimes he could recall fragments of a mansion located in Howard Beach, Queens. He had not seen it, or his family, for the longest time. As a result of his fall into the sewer, his mind carried blurred images only. Cruel frustrating images, conflicting memories, burning bright in the foul depths of his world.

But now—now there was hope for Matteo.

It had happened several times before, when the moon speared a silver shaft down through an ancient grating, fingers of light penetrating the gloom. And there he saw, set into the wall, were iron rungs.

At first, he shrank back. He always did. Dare he go back to the world above, a haunted creature, and reclaim what was his? Or would those same powerful enemies be waiting for him? Was he not safer here, in the blackness?

Matteo found himself climbing faster, hand over hand, his blackened fingers clamping each rung with greater intensity. His tongue licked along his filthy lips. Fresh air taunted his nostrils. He pressed his bearded face against the grating. He could see the sky now, the shapes of buildings.

And then the moon was blotted out.

A shoe stepped onto the grating.

A human being.

Matteo's heart soared. He let out a whimper, then another, louder. "Help me," he called. It came out a distorted gurgling sound, incomprehensible.

Whoever was standing above jumped aside. A moment later a face was looking down into his, curious eyes squinting, blinking through the grating. Matteo pushed his face hard up against the bars. His throat emptied tangled guttural sounds.

Fear wrought the stranger's face. The man let out a hideous cry of terror and ran.

"No, come back!" Matteo hurled after the disappearing footsteps.

The silence was all that was left. Tears stained his blackened cheeks. A choked sob broke from his throat. And then Matteo retreated back into the inky sewer. Back into his home. Back into his tomb. Where he reigned supreme.

—————•≡—————

Mike Rader is a pseudonym of Australian author and poet James Aitchison. As James Lee, Aitchison writes children's mystery and horror books for middle reader. These books are bestsellers in Asia with sales topping three million copies. As Mike Rader and JJ Munro, he writes noir crime and horror. As David Carrick, he writes radio drama. In total, Aitchison has 181 books in print. His Rader and Munro short stories have been published by Akashic Books, and appeared in Horror Tree, Massacre Magazine, and Gathering Storm Magazine.

Sometimes staying dead can be difficult.

The Field of Horrors

Michael D. Davis

He shot Eve Ackery four times. Three in the stomach and once in the head. She fell where she stood, in a barren old field in the middle of nowhere. He looked at her as she took her last breath before he got back in the car and left.

Eve had been twenty-five. Now she was a body with her mouth agape and her eyes staring at the clouds rolling over the sky. They were the first to go, her beautiful celery green eyes. Birds pecked them from her skull as she lay sleeping the big sleep.

The night clouds broke loose, and rain came down with a fury. Watered-down blood trickled over the curves of Eve's face as rain filled her mouth and eye sockets. The rain kept the bugs away from her that night, though some ants floated in the pools of her eyes.

The next morning a squirrel drank some water from her lips and was scared off by a hissing noise. A shadow dropped over Eve, roaming over her entire body at a fast pace. The turkey vulture landed next to her head and looked at her with a grin spreading over his beak. Others soon joined.

Six months later there wasn't much left to poor Eve. She had turned black with decay; those were the parts the animals and bugs didn't get first. It was early spring; weeds and grass grew up around her like a fence around her home.

After a night of spring showers, in the fertile ground that took Eve Ackery, a small pink seedling popped up. The tiny thing pulsed and grew each day. It didn't take long for buds to form as it stretched upward.

It grew like a vine twisting up through the middle of her decomposed body. Always with a constant *thump, thump, thump* pulsing through its stalk. Long enough, the vine coiled slowly around one of Eve's ribs. The vine reached for another, then another. Soon, most of her dirty, dead bones were knitted together with the pinkish-white vine.

Eve's skull was the last to be enveloped. It twisted around her face slowly, rebuilding it. The vine brought back her lips, nose, ears, and lastly her eyes.

She took her breath like it was her first. Eve's eyes burnt when she opened them. She started to cry involuntarily; the tears stopped the burning. She sat up, looking at her tanned, naked skin. She had little hair on her body, like a newborn baby.

Eve ran her hands over her torso, chest, and head. There was nothing wrong. No scars, nothing. Even her thigh tattoo was gone. Eve stood up. The grass was knee high. She turned around once, twice, then took a step. She felt something underfoot. It was her shoe, one of them.

Chewed, rotten, dirty, horrible smelling, but wearable. She wrapped a part of her jeans that were embedded in the ground around her other foot and started walking.

A few yards away sat a gravel road. Eve followed it for a few hours before hitting a crossroads. She headed north, but stopped not long after. A rumbling noise came from over a small hill, then a cloud of dust. An old Ford pickup slammed to a stop when it saw the naked Eve standing on the gravel road. Eve sauntered over to the pickup, a shiver going up her spine in the hot weather.

Tyler Clearman was just shy of forty. He had some of his teeth and a bald spot he didn't like to talk about. But this was the best day he had all week, he thought as he saw Eve.

"May I have a ride into town?" Eve said to Tyler through the old-fashioned roll-down window.

"Depends. What do I get for my trouble? Town's all the way back there, and I don't wanna make the trip if I'm not gonna get somethin' for it." Tyler grinned his swiss cheese grin.

Eve didn't move or respond. Tyler took it as a yes and reached out the window, touching Eve's boob. Tyler had taken it wrong. Eve grabbed him at the elbow then slammed his head down on the door frame. Tyler's nose suddenly looked like a red water fountain. Eve opened the door and dragged Tyler to the gravel. She kicked him in the face with her shoed foot when he squirmed. Then he laid still.

Eve took his jacket, put it on, got in the truck, hung a U-ey, and headed toward town. The cab stunk. She changed the radio from country western to some oldies and used all eight cylinders on her journey.

Hinchley was a small town. Eve hadn't been a resident of it long before the incident. She had moved there with him. And two months later he'd done this to her.

Eve pulled up outside a thrift store and checked the jacket pockets. There was a cellphone and a wallet with about eighty-five dollars in it. She waited until a kid of about ten started to skateboard past.

"Hey, kid," Eve said, "wanna make twenty bucks?"

"How?" asked the kid, keeping a safe distance away.

"I give you ten bucks and you go in there get me some clothes. You keep the change and this twenty."

"That's it?"

"That's it."

He thought it over then agreed. Eve wrote down what she needed on the back of a burger receipt and the kid went in. Not long after he came out holding a bag full of clothes. She paid him and he left. Jeans, an ironic black shirt with a skull on it and a pair of sneakers that actually looked pretty good were in the bag. After dressing in the truck, Eve went into the store grabbed a hat to cover her bald head and some cheap sunglasses.

After changing, she started the truck, put on her hat and glasses, then pulled away from the curb. Eve knew where she was going. It didn't take her long to get there.

She parked the truck down the street and started walking to the house. Their house, her house.

Eve was coming up on the grass and making a beeline straight for the front door when it opened. She ducked behind a tree, fast.

He stood there, talking to a woman who held a baby.

"I'm sorry," he said, "if I don't work we don't live."

"Then maybe we just won't live," she said. "Zombies are very popular these days."

"But then I'm gonna have to work to put brains on the table." He smiled, she laughed. "Anyways, I couldn't do that to our little man."

"He is beautiful, isn't he?"

"Of course he is, and you're a beautiful mommy."

"And you're a handsome daddy."

They kissed.

Eve felt like killing all three of them. She watched as he walked to his car and drove away. Hot tears formed in the corners of her eyes. How long had it been? Days? Weeks? Years? Eve remembered the phone in the jacket pocket and grabbed it, checking the date. A scream formed in her throat. A year. It had been a year, just over a year.

Eve wiped her eyes. There was no time to think about it. A year was gone; she would deal with it later. At the present moment she had other problems to deal with.

Back at the truck, Eve pulled the back of the seat forward. A metal toolbox sat behind the driver's side; a shotgun rested on the passenger's side. She pulled out the gun and checked it. It was loaded. Tyler Clearman came prepared. Eve put the shotgun on the seat and grabbed a foot-long wrench out of the toolbox.

Eve got something to eat then swung past the store for some duct tape. She had moved here because of him. He got a job down here at the factory after crashing on Eve's couch for who knows how long. Eve quit her job and followed him because he told her to come. He was that kind of guy. There was a part of her that didn't want to move, but there were times when being with him almost made it worth it. She didn't want to give up on him; he wasn't the worst. Eve almost smiled at the thought. She never should have come to this town.

At the back corner of the parking lot, next to the woods, Eve waited. She had a perfect view of the front door to the factory and of his car. Hours crawled by, and Eve sweated gallons in the truck.

The shift was getting out and men and women flowed from the building. She saw him going straight for his car. Eve called his name as she got out of the truck. He looked around but didn't see her. She clutched the wrench behind her arm and called to him again.

His eyes were almost as big as CDs. He ran toward her and the truck. She led him to the truck's rear at the back edge of the parking lot. Trees bordered the area and surrounded the truck, blocking the view to anyone remaining in the lot.

"You're dead. You can't be. Who are you? Who! Who are you?" He yelled.

Eve said, "The woman you killed."

"This is impossible," he muttered as Eve brought the wrench up to the side of his head. His shoulders slammed down on the open tailgate and Eve quickly snatched his legs and swung him up and in. She hit him again with the wrench and he was out cold. Eve taped him up fast, put up the gate, and drove off.

She found the field easily, almost like she was drawn to it. The night had gotten dark on the drive, so she left the headlights on when she stopped. Eve dropped him from the truck and smiled at his pained moans muffled by the duct tape. She dragged him through grass, weeds, and dirt. Bathed in the truck's headlights, he laid in the spot where Eve had died. The spot where he had killed her. Eve tore the tape from his face, taking some skin with it, and dropped it in the dirt.

When he was done screaming in pain, he yelled, "What is this, you bitch?"

Eve just stood there, holding the shotgun as he bellowed.

"I shot you! You were dead!"

"I was dead," Eve said, "and soon you will be too."

"What? What!"

"You hit me, bruised me, hurt me more times than I can count. That one time, and you know the time I mean, you even raped me. I've never said that before. Never admitted it."

"That's not true, you bitch!"

"I just hate that it took a bullet to the head for me to say so and to do what I should have done a long time ago."

"Yeah, what's that?"

"Kill you," Eve pointed the gun at his head. "See you next year," she said and pulled the trigger.

Eve left the truck in a parking lot. When Tyler saw it, he picked it up without complaint. He didn't report it stolen because being thrown out of his own truck by a naked woman wasn't something he wanted to go around telling.

Eve stayed in town for a while and saw that he was reported missing. A search was formed, not a big one, and he wasn't found. It said in the paper he had a history of domestic abuse and infidelity and was suspected to have run off with a woman other than his wife. Learning that he had gotten married in that year just pissed Eve off more.

For a while, she went back home and took care of some things. But around eleven months after she'd shot him in that field, Eve headed back to the small town. She checked on him, and he had a nice growth but wasn't fully formed.

Over the next month she checked him about every day. It took him one year and twenty-two days to wake. When he did, Eve was sitting there a revolver in her hands.

"Eve," he said.

"You've been dead a year," she said. "Let's see you go another." She shot him in the forehead.

The year after that he woke up and she had already tied him down. She stood over him with a knife.

"How many times are you gonna do this?" He whimpered.

"How many times did you hit me?"

Then she brought the knife down, adding, "See you next year."

———————

Michael D. Davis was born and raised in a small town in Iowa. A high school graduate and avid reader he has aspired to be a writer for years. Having written over thirty short stories, ranging in genre from comedy to horror from flash fiction to novella some of which have been published in Out of the Gutter Online, Near to the Knuckle online magazine, Horla, Fiction on the Web, Sirens call, and The Dark City mystery and crime magazine. He continues in his accursed pursuit of a career in the written word and in his hunt Michael's love for stories in all genres and mediums will not falter.

Not everyone visits the cemetery to visit the departed.

Markers

Michael H. Hanson

"Every man should keep a fair-sized cemetery
in which to bury the faults of his friends."
– Henry Ward Beecher

You might call this my true home, better known as the Resurrection Cemetery. With one hundred lovely acres, it is located within an industrial park inside of Piscataway, New Jersey, a very decentralized town, and, as such, has many advantages for a person of my, um, nature.

The graves here are identified with either flat memorials or upright monuments. Wide vistas of green fields are dotted with strong trees, and a statue of the risen Christ welcomes visitors with outstretched arms.

Distant footsteps bring me back to full alert. The damn fog is messing with my echolocation and I can't tell if that bastard Vinnie is twenty feet away or two hundred. I owe him nearly ninety grand after that last series of bets at his off-the-books casino in Newark. Somehow, he followed me and managed a lucky shot—clipped my right thigh that is now slowly bleeding out.

Crypt Gnats

I stand up and crouch over, walking behind a short stretch of mausoleums. This should lead me to a row of graves where I'll have a good pick, if memory serves. My right leg almost buckles, but I grit my teeth and push on. Usually I keep myself in pretty good shape, but I guess I had just gotten too used to this body, and after four decades I'm feeling the drawbacks of being in my late sixties.

A scuffling sound off to my left makes me freeze for a full minute. I slowly let my breath out and then continue my slow walk. I squint my eyes, but this bloody fog makes it hard to keep my bearing.

For a few seconds I ponder what brought me to this desperate morning. It was the gambling, of course. My one true Achilles heel. I kept it at bay all through my marriage, but when my wife Judy died from breast cancer four years ago I found myself with too much free time on my hands. No matter how many times I've gotten a second chance at life, I always succumb to that drumming urge in my bloodstream. No matter the age, sex, or race I regenerate as, nothing can hold back that all-encompassing desire to throw caution on the line in wonderful expectation of an outcome to probability and chance forever.

A loud crack and my left shoulder burns. I stagger quickly into a thicker patch of fog and hobble in the direction I hope my pre-scouted graves are. I tap my shoulder with my right hand and gasp. It feels like a flesh wound and is not bleeding too fast. Still, I don't have much time. Vinnie's heavy breathing is too close, but I just can't figure out where he is.

A few minutes later I reach a long crest of grass. Smiling, I settle to the beginning on this ridgeline, and then my jaw drops. There isn't a stone marker in sight, just some small red flags, used by utility workers to mark gas lines that now pepper the immediate area.

Oh shit, I think. I suddenly know where I am. A full six hundred feet in the wrong direction.

"I know you're close," Vinnie shouts, sounding closer but still no easier to locate. "I can smell you, old man. You're bleeding out. But not so fast. I can have some fun with you before you croak."

My mouth is dry and the damned pounding in my ears just won't go away. I know the blasted sun is going to rise soon and then its goodbye fog and goodbye me. I grit my teeth and put all my focus in what I know is the right direction, doing my best not to shuffle too loudly, but damn it, I'm losing feeling in my right leg and can't help dragging it.

"A promise is a promise, you slimy mick," Vinnie's voice rings out, maybe closer, maybe not, "and this time ain't no cops or neighborhood watch groups gonna get between you and me, Duffy."

The next two hundred feet are an endless nightmare. I hear Vinnie's angry breathing get closer and closer. I can just start making out a bright white globe on the horizon and know everything is truly coming to a head. I totter twice but just manage to stay on my feet when I reach the row of markers I so desperately want.

A new crack. So close! A sharp pain in my right hip. I drop to my knees uncontrollably as two more gunshots follow. I hear the bullets rip through the air just where my head was a split second earlier. I fall down on my hands and knees and frantically crawl forward across the graves closest to me. Squinting, I desperately glance at names and dates cut into marble and granite.

"Sorry about that," Vinne shouts, "honestly. I was targeting your legs, but I slipped on some wet grass."

Vinnie sounds like he is about ten yards away, ready to burst out of the thick mist behind me. Then a headstone catches my eye. Angela Rinaldi, nineteen forty-five to nineteen fifty.

So young. I frown. My eyes start blurring and I know I don't have any time to crawl to any more graves. No more choices. It is now or never. Vinnie's footsteps sound about twenty-five feet away and closing.

With my last fragments of strength, I slam my wrinkled, liver-spotted right hand against the surface of the granite marker, just atop the name etched into it. The result is nearly instantaneous.

A gurgle of extreme pain erupts from my lips and my eyes fill with blinding light. I'd almost forgotten how agonizing a rebirth was for me . . . almost.

"What the fu . . ." I hear Vinnie stop in his tracks; close, but still not quite close enough to know exactly where I was.

The entire process takes about a minute.

Ectoplasmic tendrils erupt all over my body and stab downward into the soil. In seconds they find the coffin and rapidly work their way under the locked cover. My filaments pierce the corpse within in moments, flooding into bones, then deeper down, into individual cells, hungry for even the smallest particles of DNA. And then they find them.

Back atop the plot, my body crumbles into itself, as if

I have just bumped into a microscopic black hole and am being crushed into a tiny spot. Seconds later the agonizing process reverses itself, as all my former matter regenerates and starts growing new cells, multiplying at an exponential rate.

"I see you," Vinnie yells. "Now get up and let the party begin."

Holding back a grin, I force myself to whimper as I stand up. The rising sun instantly burns through the nearby patch of fog and illuminates my naked body.

"Holy Christ," Vinnie gasps.

I do my best to contort my face into an approximation of fear and confusion. Vinnie grits his teeth and looks all around as the rising sun makes the entire surrounding graveyard evident. Obviously not seeing the old man he was hunting, Vinnie stuffs his Glock into his waistband and drops to one knee in front of me.

"Honey," Vinnie says in a surprisingly gentle voice I have never heard him use before, "what are you doing here? Where are your parents? And your clothes?"

"They're dead," I let my voice waver. "I just escaped the foster home. My new daddy was hurting me. Please don't make me go back, mister. I'm so cold."

This last statement obviously cut through Vinnie's shock and he gently picks me up and starts walking. In a couple of minutes, I see his familiar Lincoln Continental. He sets me down on my feet, pops the trunk, and pulls out a grey blanket. Right before he slams it shut I get a quick glimpse of rope, duct tape, pliers, garden shears, and a small chainsaw. I'm sure he mistakes my shudders for exposure and shock.

A couple of minutes later, I'm wrapped in the blanket and sitting up in the back seat.

"Baby," Vinnie says quickly into his cell phone, "I can't explain it all right now. I got a kid. Abandoned, I think. A little girl. No I can't take her to the cops right now and don't ask me why."

I can just hear the tones of a woman coming from the phone. Tense. Worried. And maybe a touch of something more.

"I'm so hungry mister," I say loudly and plaintively.

The response is perfect. "Okay, okay," Vinnie says defensively. "I get it, you heard her. Go ahead and make your damned soup. We'll be there in about forty minutes, give or take. What?"

Vinnie turns around and looks me in the eyes. "What's your name, sweetheart?"

"Angela," I say softly.

"You got that?" Vinnie says to his phone. "Yeah? Actually, yeah, she does look Italian. Listen, I don't want no cop catching me talking on my cell phone. I'll see you soon."

"You don't worry about nothing," Vinnie says while looking at me in the rearview mirror. "My wife Sheila is gonna take real good care of you, get you cleaned up and fed and then, well . . . we'll see what happens . . . ."

I lean back against the large seat and let out a slow sigh of relief. Vinnie's tone, what I sensed in Sheila's distant voice . . . yes, I can tell this is a couple that never had kids. Nearing middle age, maybe they suffered through some miscarriages. Yes. I'd be safe with them until I grew into full womanhood and could take care of myself.

And who knows? I might even grow to like and ad-mire this hatchet man who just minutes earlier wanted to torture me to death. Once, in a previous life, I fell in love with a would-be murderer after one of these transitions and even ended up marrying her, oh, two hundred plus years ago.

Vinnie pulled onto Route 287 South and picked up speed.

"I dunno where you snuck off to Duffy," Vincent says, surprising me, though I instantly realize he is just talking to himself, "but if you don't bleed out in some ditch I am gonna get you yet."

I ponder my naked toes. All this time and I still don't know quite what I am. When I first transmogrified, I was just an English settler's boy of ten in the late fifteenth century, dying upon a Conoy burial mound not quite ten miles from where my latest ascension took place, and waking up in a Native American girl's body. Over the centuries I slowly learned about my abilities, knowing that I was not one hundred percent immortal and could definitely be hurt and die forever just like anyone else if I didn't manage to find a consecrated resting place to kick-start my ongoing actuality.

For some unknown reason, this power of mine did not work near a common, unsanctioned grave, mortuary, or freshly killed body. I've tested this supposition far too many times in the course of the multiple lifetimes I have traveled all over the Earth. I can only induce a rebirth in the hallowed soil of the land that eventually became the boundaries that mark Piscataway, New Jersey. What religion or belief doesn't matter—Christian, Jew, Muslim, Hindu, Buddhist, whatever.

Crypt Gnats

Am I demon? Damned soul? Of extraterrestrial origin? Something other? I simply do not know. I've earned numerous academic degrees over the centuries and spent decades researching my own anatomy, but always to no end. My abilities are beyond the study and detection of religion, technology, philosophy, and science. I have had multiple spouses, both men and women, over the course of my many lifetimes, and yes, I loved them all and grieved their eventual passing in my own way.

One major regret that I carry into all of my futures is that I'm cursed with infertility. I can neither father children nor ever get pregnant. I occasionally resorted to adoption, but the last time was so many years ago that no one I have ever called son or daughter currently endures.

In time I finally decided to simply accept the macabre nature of my existence and to just live and enjoy my eldritch life. Unfortunately, I often take that philosophy too far, especially when it comes to my penchant for gambling. No matter if I am man or woman, Caucasian or African or Asian, my desire to challenge the gods of chance is always there, just waiting to erupt.

Vinnie pulls onto Route 95 North and pushes it up to seventy miles an hour. Already, I can feel the memories of a former lifetime ease their way into the background of my real-time thoughts. As with all of my former rebirths, a multitude of recollections of this new body's past experience endure in this brain. They will inform much of my being from now on, and falling into the emotional mindset of a young girl will be as exhilarating as it is alien. It is the blessing and curse that I always choose to embrace.

The sky is a beautiful mix of blue sky and white clouds.

Crypt Gnats

The future offers up several promises of days to come and, you know, they are pretty appealing. Halloween trick or treating. Christmas morning presents. Hunting for eggs on Easter. Birthday parties. Making neighborhood and school friends.

Exhausted, I slowly lean against the door and fall asleep.

Life is good.

———◆———

Author Michael H. Hanson created the ongoing Sha'daa shared-world anthology series Sha'daa: Tales of the Apocalypse, Sha'daa: Last Call, Sha'daa: Pawns, Sha'daa: Facets, Sha'daa: Inked, and Sha'daa: Toys. Michael's short story C.H.A.D. appeared in C.H.U.D. Lives! His short story Rock and Road appeared in Shadows and Reflections, and his short story Born of Dark Waters appeared in the The Beauty Of Death 2: Death By Water anthology. Michael also has stories in Janet Morris's Heroes in Hell (HIH) anthology volumes Lawyers In Hell, Rogues In Hell, Dreamers In Hell, Poets In Hell, Doctors In Hell, Pirates In Hell, and Lovers In Hell. Michael has had over 100 short stories published in the fields of horror, science fiction, and fantasy.

*A cemetery isn't always the best place
to meet girls.*

Ghoulfriend

David Perlmutter

Gary knew he shouldn't be going outside to the cemetery so late at night, but he wasn't afraid. He knew that most of the talk he'd heard about the place was just that: talk. In all his sixteen years, he'd often wondered how it could even be possible that there was the kind of life after death that he was being warned about.

Besides, if there *was* such a thing in the cemetery, living after death, then he knew he wouldn't be alone. He had relatives there who had passed on, so he found an odd sort of comfort in the place.

Sitting on a stone bench next to his aunt's grave, he heard a voice.

"Hey!" it said.

Gary turned around.

It was a girl, about his age, but she was bigger and looked stronger than he was. While he was dressed in long sleeved clothes for protection against the chill, she sported a sleeveless shirt. Her hair was black and short, and her eyes were black as well. Her face had a sour and menacing expression that he typically only saw in girls when they were angry, so he guessed he had offended her by his presence. Still, there was something in her that somehow made her attractive in a certain way he could not explain. He stared at her intently. At least until she saw him doing it.

"What are you looking at?" she growled.

Gary struggled to find the right words to say. I . . . uh . . . ."

"Don't bother!" she said, cutting him off. "I know your type. You got lost on your way home, and you need help getting back. Well, don't ask me to lead you there, dumbass. You bumbled your way here, and by the looks of it, you can just bumble your way out of it again."

"I'm not lost!" Gary said, in defense of his honor. "And I'm not dumb, either. I wanted to come here."

She laughed.

"Wanted to come here?" she exclaimed. "That's a new one."

"Sure. I come here every chance I get."

"You're not serious."

"I am. I don't feel like I fit anywhere else. Communing with the deceased gives me a feeling that there's an existence beyond life."

"Cut out that crap!" she ordered.

"Huh?" he answered.

"Being dead ain't no better than being alive. It's the same sort of crap as being alive, except you get told you don't matter at all, and you can't have the kind of 'real' life the living people always have."

"And how would *you* know what being dead is like?"

"Because I am dead, you moron!"

Gary suddenly realized his life was in peril, even though he was not entirely certain why. He shivered, and not from the cold.

"Yeah," the girl responded, cynically. "That's the usual response."

"What are you?" he said. "A zombie?"

"No. I still have my *brains*, so I'm not one of *those* losers. I'm a *ghoul*."

"A what?"

"Don't you know what that is?"

"Should I?"

"I would think that somebody who hangs around haunted places like this one would know of my kind intimately."

"Not me. I've never seen a ghoul before in my life."

"Fine. Here's what a ghoul does."

She went over to him and whispered into his ear.

He withdrew from her in even greater fear than before. "That's disgusting!" he snapped. "These places are supposed to be where the dead are respected and honored. Not anything like what *you* do to them."

She suddenly grabbed him aggressively by the arm with strength he found impossible to resist.

"I figured you for one of those hypocrite humans the moment you came in!" she snapped. "Paint me as a monster, will ya? I'm just trying to get sustenance the only way I know how. And it ain't like you guys are all the way innocent about what you eat, either! Think about all those animals you slaughter, those plants you put in the ground, the tree fruit you scavenge. It's not like we're any different than you."

As she dropped his arm, Gary suddenly felt ashamed of himself for condemning her, knowing that she had a point. "Listen . . . uh . . . ."

"Bronwen. If you must know."

"Bronwen, I'm sorry about insulting your . . . diet. I shouldn't have . . . .

"Wouldn't have expected you to know from the start . . . uh . . . ."

"Gary."

"The thing is, Gary, you got to understand is that we so-called 'creatures of the night' ain't all the things you make us out to be. And, to be honest, you've convinced me that you humans ain't all judgmental jerks either."

"Really?"

"Besides, I actually think that I kind of like you . . . in that dumb old romantic way you humans have of looking at each other. You being all handsome and all."

Gary blushed, "You think so? Well, honestly . . . I was kind of attracted to you to begin with. None of the other girls I know want to be near this place. They don't . . . understand . . . ."

"I do, buddy. I always will."

To his surprise, she started kissing him. He kissed her back. They embraced, tenderly . . . then she punched him in the face with so much power that he fell to the ground, paralyzed with hurt and pain.

He struggled as she strangled him, and then she stopped. He couldn't breathe, his windpipe was crushed, and he stared at her in confusion and terror. He gasped like a fish on land, unable to take in air. His world was growing black, but he could still feel as she bit into his side and pulled off a chunk of flesh. He wanted to scream, but he couldn't get the breath, so he lay on his aunt's grave, silently choking to death, and bleeding out as he heard her chewing, loudly.

She swallowed, patted the top of his head, and said, "I knew you'd fall for it. You teenage boys are so horny . . . and so gullible!"

He watched her go in for another bite and silently sobbed as she laughed. "And you all have such good meat on you, too."

David Perlmutter is a freelance writer based in Winnipeg, Manitoba, Canada. He is the author of America Toons In: A History of Television Animation The Singular Adventures Of Jefferson Ball, The Pups, Certain Private Conversations and Other Stories, Honey and Salt, Orthicon; or, the History of a Bad Idea, The Encyclopedia of American Animated Television Shows and Let's Be Buddies. His short stories can be read on Curious Fictions at Curious Fictions/David Perlmutter. He can be reached on Facebook at David Perlmutter-Writer, Twitter at @DKPLJW1, and Tumblr at The Musings of David Perlmutter (yesdavidperlmutterfan).

Sometimes the word on the street should be looked into carefully.

The Ginger Man

Jeff Dosser

Sean took a drag on his blunt and exhaled into the smoky atmosphere of the Camaro's narrow cab. "So you're tellin' me"—he waved a freckled arm towards the old brick building at the end of the lot—"there's thousands ah dollars inside?"

His best friend, Micha, smacked the steering wheel and rocked back in his seat. **"Bitch, that's** what I'm sayin'." Micha shook his head, his dreadlocks bouncing like springs. "Ain't no one round here not heard 'bout the crazy ol' woman what lives in there an' her treasure hid inside."

"Well I never heard 'bout it," Sean complained. He handed Micha the blunt and took a sip of beer. "How in the world would some homeless chick come up with thousands ah bucks? An' if she did, why would she live there?"

"Cause she crazy," Micha wheezed, taking a toke and doing his best to hold it down. After several seconds he puffed out a gray cloud and rolled down the window.

"Back in the seventies," Micha said, "this place was

78

makin' money hand over fist. Then that bitch's ol' man got popped by the cops when all them street people was disappearin' 'round town." He nodded towards the building. "Guy committed suicide right in there. Burned hisself up in the basement ovens."

"Whad'ya mean, basement ovens?" Sean asked.

"Place was a funeral parlor, homes. They embalmed bodies and cremated people in there. What you think that big ass chimney fo' anyhow?"

Sean leaned forward and squinted into the gloom. The abandoned mortuary was a single-story brick structure with chain-wrapped double doors and metal-barred windows. At the far end of the building, a looming stone chimney jutted up like a gravestone.

"But you ain't said nothin' 'bout the money," Sean said. "How'd some homeless chick get so much cash?"

"Well, she weren't always homeless an' crazy." Micha rolled his eyes. "It weren't till the IRS took all her shit that she moved into the funeral home. Bitch had no place ta go. When she moved in, she took everythin' them government boys couldn't lay their hands on. Cash and jewelry, that kinda thing."

"So how you know she rich?" Sean asked. "Maybe she was broke an' didn't have nothin' left."

Micha pursed his lips. "Mm, mm, mm. Boy, you ain't lived round here long nuff to learn much 'bout this city." He turned and jerked his head towards downtown. "You know that ol' mansion on Cherry Street? The one with all them flashin' lights at Christmas?"

Sean's eyes drifted to the ceiling in thought. "You mean the ol' Blackstone mansion?"

"That's the one," Micah said. He raised an arm and pointed to an old woman crossing the street and entering the lot. She hunched over a shopping cart loaded with junk, her gaunt frame rounded by layers of filthy clothes. "Meet Miss Emma Blackstone."

Sean stared into twilight's deepening shadows at what appeared to be just another homeless old woman. "Shit, how you know that's Emma Blackstone?"

"Man, everyone know her," Micha said. "Momma told all us kids, 'You stay 'way from that Blackstone funeral parlor. That Blackstone woman a witch.' Course Momma just tryin' ta keep us kids from breakin' in an' shit. Hell, that what everyone tell their kids round here. Stay 'way from that Blackstone place, she gonna grab ya and toss ya in the oven."

The old woman trundled her cart up to the side of the building and parked it beneath the chimney.

"My aunt, "Micah said, "told me that on full moons, you can see the souls of lost children twistin' in the smoke comin' from that chimney." He gripped the wheel and stared into the night, his voice distant and low. "She says when ya see 'em, they smell just like cinnamon." He shrugged and looked to Sean. "Least ways, that's what Aunt Lakeisha says."

Sean rolled his eyes. "This the same crack ho aunt turnin' tricks down on 11th?"

Micha shrugged. "Yeah, but that don't mean she's wrong."

Sean studied the old woman and the building. Finally, he said, "If she's so rich an' got all that money an' jewels inside, why don't we just grab her an' beat it outta her?"

"'Cause she's also batshit crazy," Micha said. "You ever get up next ta her an' all she do is babble. Hell, she can't even form a sentence that makes no sense."

"Then how the hell we supposed ta find her stash?" Sean asked. "That's a pretty goddamn big building. It could be anywhere."

"'Cause I got this." He pulled a sheet of paper from his pocket and unfolded it before passing it to Sean. It was a page torn from a journal. The paper was yellowed and brittle along the edges. At the top, printed in a neat, flowing script it read:

Nov 1, 1 a.m.

Feeling much better after last night's meeting. Still having trouble sleeping, but the nightmares seem to be letting up. I think the medicine might be helping.

I've been worried about the jewelry all week. I'm afraid I'll forget where I'm going to hide it so I'm recording it in my journal. Hopefully, I'll remember to look in here.

Below this was a drawing of a building with an arrow pointing to a room in the North West corner. Beneath the arrow was printed:

Urns—second shelf. Diamonds are in the one labeled john fike, the rest in the urn labeled samantha whippet.

"How'd you get this?" Sean asked handing back the page.

Micha laughed and stuffed the paper in his pocket. "Luck, plain dumb luck."

Sean brushed a lock of long red hair from his eyes and stared. "Well? You gonna tell me or ain't ya?"

Micha grinned and went on. "Two days ago, me, Lil' Kee, an' Peanut was all standin' round shootin' the shit when crazy ol' Blackstone come walkin' cross the lot. Course we didn't pay her no attention until we hear her rantin' and ravin', yellin' all kinda weird shit." He leaned back in the seat, his face taking on a dreamy, faraway look. "Her voice seemed ta come from everywhere an' nowhere all at the same time." He looked to Sean and blinked, like a man waking from a dream. "Then she take this book outta her basket an' start rippin' out pages an' chuckin' 'em in the air."

Headlights turned onto the road where they were parked and they ducked down, waiting for them to pass. Micha pushed up in his seat and checked the rearview mirror before going on.

"Anyway, it was windy as hell an' them pages come dancin' crost the parkin' lot, like drunken white birds, swirled round us like leaves. Then this one here," Micha tapped his pocket and smiled, "stuck to my leg. So I pull it off an' take a look. I don't have ta tell ya I seen immediately what I had."

"I always said you was one lucky bastard," Sean said. "But why you pick me to go with ya? Why don't you just go in yourself an' get them jewels?"

Micha paused and stared through the windshield. He watched as the old woman sifted through her belongings. "You my best friend, man. I thought we'd share."

Sean stared at him for a long while. "Shiiiit, man. You're scared."

"I ain't scared ah nothin'!" Micha snarled.

"You scared ah all them witch stories your momma

tol' when you was a kid," Sean laughed. "Oh brother, that's rich."

"You want a piece of this or not?" Micha said angrily. "I can call Peanut an' he'll be down here in a minute."

"Naw, man. I'm just yankin' your chain." Sean nodded towards the building. "How we supposed ta get in there anyway? Place is locked up tight."

"Just watch," Micha said. He grew quiet, leaning forward and gripping the wheel.

For several minutes, the old woman rummaged in her basket, taking out this and that. Suddenly she straightened. Her eyes scanned the area, pausing long enough on their car to have both boys sliding down in their seats. Then with an agility unexpected in one so old, she dropped to her knees and disappeared from sight.

"Where'd she go?" Sean asked.

"Come on," Micha said. He opened the door and stepped out. "I'll show ya."

Sean followed as they jogged across the lot.

"Man, pull up your hoodie," Micha said glancing over. "Ain't no one gonna notice another brother runnin' down the street, but people remember a red-haired white boy." He laughed. "'Specially one as pale as you."

When they reached the building, Sean spotted a metal grate covering a hole in the wall near the bottom. Micha pulled out two flashlights and handed one to Sean.

"I've been watchin' her since I found that note," Micha said. "I figure we follow the old bat inside, tie her up an' grab her stash."

"Just tie her up, right?"

"Yeah, man. We ain't gonna hurt her. Just don't want

her sneakin' up on us with a blade or somethin' while we lookin' round."

Micha dropped to his knees and with a wide-eyed glance at Sean, scrambled inside.

The crawl space beneath the building smelled of mold and rust, the powdery dry soil cool against Sean's hands. In the pale glow of their lights, a battered rectangular air duct dangled from above, ramping down to the dirt floor.

"That must be how she gets in," Micha whispered. He played his light across the two-foot tunnel of ductwork snaking into the darkness.

"You first," Sean said. He gulped down a chill he couldn't explain and cast a doubtful eye to the dim square of fading light leading to the outside lot. All at once, a treasure hunt didn't sound like such a good idea.

Micha wormed his way inside, the duct work popping with tinny metallic pings as he went. Sean waited for Micha's light to disappear before following him in.

"You back there?" Micha's voice echoed.

"Yeah, man. Right behind ya."

Sean followed the pops and pings of his friend's progress until his knees grew sore and the aluminum rivets dug painfully into his palms.

"Dude, how far?"

Silence.

"Micha?"

Sean crept forward, pausing at a T-intersection before clicking off his light and straining into the darkness for any sign of Micha. A metallic clatter, like that of pans, drew his eye to the left. Not more than a dozen feet away, a sickly glow seeped from a vented grill and painted the dull aluminum walls.

Sean crept closer.

Eye pressed to the vent, he stared down on what had to be a kitchen. Three steel topped tables shimmered beneath a naked bulb's yellow beams; the walls lined with dust-covered boxes and rusted metal shelves. On the back wall, a rack of knives glittered.

Then Sean caught sight of the crib. He swallowed, the sound a dry click in the back his throat.

A faded yellow blanket marred with a reddish-brown stain was draped over the crib's corner. But it wasn't the blanket or the ancient crib that filled him with dread. It was the mobile dangling above. Unlike his niece's mobile, with its bright twirling zebras and bouncing orange giraffes, this mobile was hung with gleaming knives and cookie cutters whose silvery edges shimmered with razor keen sharpness. As he watched, the mobile began to turn, the sour notes of a broken lullaby seeping through the room.

Heart pounding, Sean thumped along the duct, not caring where Micha had gone, not caring for the money, not caring about anything but finding a way out.

Suddenly, the vent buckled beneath him. He slid down, tumbling out of the tube and landing with a thump on a hard metal grate. Before his light flickered out and sank him into darkness, he was covered in an explosion of gray powder.

Sean sat up, bumping his head on the low ceiling. He licked his lips and felt around. The powder covering him was sweet. He rubbed a finger across a dusty cheek and stuck it in his mouth. Sweet like sugar but with a spicy bite. Cinnamon?

What the hell's going on? Sean's heart thundered as he ran his hands along each wall. There was no opening, no exit.

A warm orange glow at the end of his confined space caught his eye, a circular window the size of a fist with light just beyond. As he crawled across the grating to peer out, a face appeared on the other side. The face of a crook-nosed old woman. She held a candle in one hand and pressed a bright eye against the glass.

"Well, I'll be," she said. "A ginger ginger."

The metal grating became suddenly hot beneath Sean's hands. The cramped room filled with a cherry red glow. Then before the flames and searing pain exploded and plunged him into darkness, he heard the old woman cackled.

"A real ginger ginger."

***

Sean awoke to a world of freakish dimensions. He stared up at a gigantic light bulb dangling from a ceiling hundreds of feet above. To his left, a fist sized drop of water dangled from a faucet two stories high. He tried to sit up, to move his arms or legs, but they were frozen, immobile. Almost as if they were encased in plaster.

"Ah, you're done," a gravelly voice boomed. An ancient face of colossal proportions hovered above him. Ella Blackstone's milky gray eyes, close set above a hawkish nose and flabby wet lips, studied him with wolfish intensity.

"Nothing like fresh baked right out of the oven," she

said. Crooked pale fingers the size of tree trunks wrapped around his waist and hoisted him in the air.

This is not happening, Sean thought. *I'm dreaming.*

He strained to look down, his head pressing against unseen restraints. A gingerbread man was lying on a metal baking pan, far below. A gingerbread man that resembled Micha. A cookie whose face held the baked-on expression of terror.

The old woman shuffled across a room of vast proportions and dropped into a worn recliner. In her other hand she held a glass of milk the size of a refrigerator. For a moment she dangled Sean above the white surface.

It's a dream, Sean told himself. *A nightmare.*

His leg was dipped into the icy cold fluid before he was lifted out, and her teeth sank into his flesh. Any notion of being a dream vanished in the crimson wave of agony when his leg was nibbled off at the knee.

With a wink and a promise to finish, she set Sean down and picked up a book. Licking a nub of a pencil with her long, forked tongue, she began scratching across the page, mumbling as she wrote:

Nov 1, 1 a.m.

Feeling much better after last night's meeting. Still having trouble sleeping, but the nightmares seem to be letting up . . .

——•——

Award-winning author, Jeff Dosser, is an ex-Tulsa cop and current software developer living in the wilds of central Oklahoma. Jeff's short stories can be found in magazines such as The Literary Hatchet, Tales to

Crypt Gnats

Terrify, Shotgun Honey and Iridium Zine, to name a few. His novels, Shattered and Neverland were the 2019 and 2018 Oklahoma Writer's Federation winners for best new horror, and his sci-fi short, The Late Dawn of a Solar Knight was an L.R. Hubbard Writers of the Future Honorable Mention.

When not writing, Jeff can be found prowling the woods behind his rural home community with the denizens of the night.

Find out what Jeff's been up to on his website: jeffdosser. com or follow him on Twitter@jeffdosser

Even when you are broke, there's got to be easier ways to make ends meet.

The Grue

Dan Lee

You are likely to be eaten.

The cryptic words were scratched almost illegibly into the masonry of the mausoleum above the heavy iron door. It was the sort of warning I should have listened to as I lay in the thick, wet grass in front of the ancient sepulcher at the heart of the city cemetery.

Moss and kudzu had swallowed the outer walls and dangled in a leafy curtain over the weathered stone edifice and the rusted hinges that bled red-brown stains onto the dingy gray. The door was covered in an indecipherable mess of decayed graffiti and weathered epitaphs that had told the story of the Southern aristocrat who lay inside.

He'd been the founder of our quiet little burg, the last remnant of the sprawling plantation that had given birth to the township after the Civil War had ended. But, despite his stature, few cared enough about the history of the place to be bothered to even maintain the grave. Inside were the decrepit and likely skeletonized remains, entombed with treasures of jewelry in the fashion of the day. It was an antiquarian's wet dream and my last chance to save my home from foreclosure.

The plan had been so simple, so ingenious, I was surprised no one had ever attempted it. Under cover of darkness, long after the gates had closed and the feeble old caretaker had returned to the tenement at the far end of the property to drink himself to sleep, I would pry open the door of the crypt and make out with whatever riches had been buried inside. A pawn broker I knew a few counties over had promised to discreetly fence them for me for a cut of the profits. It was a perfect, victimless crime, after all. If not for a small placard beside the overgrown and poorly kept grave, no one would even have known the man's name, let alone the legacy attached to him. I'd be taking what had long since gone to waste and putting it to good use.

I'd been studying the job for over a week, learning the fastest way through the tombstones to my prize and the clandestine paths that would help me escape when my work was finished. I waited for the caretaker to make his final rounds, watched as he surreptitiously checked every last lock, latch, and gate. Bent and white haired, as frail as some of the corpses who slept under our feet, he was a superstitious old man who shied away from the mausoleum unless he had no choice. I hid in the blanket of kudzu until his off-key whistling had faded into the distant night before I went to work.

The door was unlocked, cracked slightly with a whisper of mildew and stale air seeping through the narrow slit. It would make my job that much easier and keep me from wrenching my back prying it open. Smiling at my good fortune, I turned on my flashlight and slipped quietly inside. The air was stale and moldy with just a hint of wet ancient earth and rot that a windowless, lightless room holding a corpse would naturally have. There were three crypts arrayed in a triangle in the room; one at each wall and a third in the center near the door. He'd had two brothers, unmarried, who had died some years before him and were buried at either side.

I started with the casket in the middle.

The lid was marked with a name and an epitaph, both weathered and illegible with a fragment of poetry talking about a "light of salvation" under the family crest. For a brief moment I felt guilty, saddened at the thought that a man could be so completely forgotten and discarded. The crowbar in my hands felt somehow heavier, more unwieldy than it actually was with that sudden burst of conscience.

The kudzu that had covered the outer walls had also crept in through the cracks in the mortar and formed a leafy carpet over the marble floor that snagged my foot and caused me to lose my balance. I caught myself on the edge of the tomb before I fell and straightened up. My palms were starting to sweat as I contemplated my job, weighed the morality and my own internal damnation at the thought of crossing that line. Once I chose to take this route, there'd be no going back. I would be a grave robber until the end of my days. The thought of the desiccated nightmare waiting for me inside only added to my fear, to the throbbing of my pulse in my ears and the burning sensation tingling up my back and through my chest. I could almost hear my father's voice in my head telling me not to do this, to show some dignity.

Then I thought about losing the house, about the bank foreclosing and taking everything from me. I thought of my wife and family leaving me, of dying destitute and alone. The fear of my impending poverty made it much easier to pry the lid from the coffin. It came off with a bump, slipped down and shattered in a thunderclap across floor. Ears ringing, I steadied myself and shined the light inside. After a few minutes I ventured a glance.

Empty!

There was nothing! No jewels, no unimaginable riches, not even the mummified corpse of some stuffed shirt who died a hundred years ago, nothing but rotting linen, dust and cobwebs. It was a hollow pine box inside an even larger stone box. I

It seemed like poetic justice, almost, to have my hopes die in an empty crypt. Swinging the crowbar into the coffin, I began to hack away at the rock and plaster, screaming so loud that I hardly even noticed the sound of stone grinding on stone behind me. From the second crypt, the lid began to shift and move. There was a tinkling of metal, a putrid air that quickly stung my nostrils and stopped me dead in my tracks.

Lifting the flashlight, I slowly pivoted around and found two gold rings lying on the floor by my feet. Tracing my way up along the kudzu and marble, the dust and shattered debris, the light rose to the open container behind me.

Eyes peered at me through the darkness, great red eyes the color of fresh blood that glowed in the night.

I should have run.

The scream was deafening as the light flashed across wet, black skin. It was the roar of a wounded predator that left my ears ringing. Red eyes reflected in the dim orange light; white teeth glistened. Pain ripped through my chest and back simultaneously as the thing in the crypt leapt on top of me and began to slash away with razor claws and slathering fangs. My skull cracked into the floor and rattled my teeth. The flashlight tumbled end over end before landing with a splash and a clatter in the blood oozing from my chest and arms. The beam of diluted light flickered once across my face, again over the face of the monster, my killer. The creature screamed again and leapt off into the shadows.

Pain gave way to nausea, further slipped into a throbbing, warbling distortion of sound and feeling in my skull as I dragged myself towards the open door of the mausoleum. Rainbow tinted explosions of light crackled and exploded in the corners of my eyes as darkness crept in from all sides.

The ringing in my ears deafened me as I closed my eyes and drifted away.

***

I woke up in the cool damp grass of the cemetery with the night watchman tending to my wounds by the light of a kerosene lantern. He'd cut away my shirt, bandaged my chest, and was cleaning the blood from my face as I struggled to move.

"Lucky to be alive," he told me, wrapping a bandage around my head. "Just lie still a minute."

"What happened?" I asked weakly.

"You learned yourself a lesson about grave robbing." The old man's words were bitter.

"And that thing? Oh God, that thing in the crypt. What was it?"

"Something best left forgotten about." The answer was cold, cryptic as he helped me sit and lean against a nearby tombstone. My chest was on fire, head pounding as I tried to focus on the old man's face. He pulled a wad of cash from his pocket and slid it into my hand. It was heavy, thick, bound in a piece of twine. He pulled me to my feet and dusted the bits of grass and debris from my back and the seat of my pants.

"I'd have just let it have you but the owners, my bosses, are too softhearted for that," he said. "They'd prefer it if no one knew about our friend there. Want to keep people from snooping around here with cameras and stupid notions like that. This is a place of quiet repose and dignity, after all."

"So what's this?" I asked, holding up the wad of cash.

"That's what you were looking for, isn't it?" he snarled. "Just keep your damn mouth shut and no one will ask where you got that money or why you were loitering around here after dark. Grave robber's an ugly title, you know?"

I nodded and tucked the money into my pocket. Together we walked out of the cemetery. I was limping a bit as he helped me along the broken gravel path towards the main gate. With every step I could feel eyes burrowing into the back of my head, hungry, wanton eyes longingly searching for me as I slowly made my escape.

"Don't look back." The old man told me, feeling me start to fidget. "He hates the light. That's why I carry the lantern. Even so, I don't know if it'll be enough to shield us both if you taunt him."

Pushing me a bit through the heavy iron gates, he wasted no time locking me out on the sidewalk.

"Do yourself a favor, son, and don't come back until it's your time."

———◆———

Dan Lee is an author, editorialist, and podcaster who works in the horror and macabre community covering news and events. He is the head writer at 52 Weeks of Horror, a contributing author with PDI Press, and co-producer of the Nashville Zombie Walk. You can find him on social media at @dotdblog.

His most recent publishing credits include stories in Noirlathotep: Tales of Lovecraftian Crime, Noirlathotep 2: More Tales of Lovecraftian Crime, and American Carnage: Tales of Trumpian Dystopia.

A good want ad covers all the details.

Help Wanted

Marcus Vance

EXTERNAL AFFAIRS CARETAKER OF SLEEPY HILL CEMETERY
Sleepy Hill has been owned by Victor Sleepy & Sons for centuries. This family-oriented funeral service seeks to provide a safe resting place for the restless deceased.

GENERAL SUMMARY
We are currently seeking a motivated individual who is passionate about the field of funerary services; someone committed to ensuring that people put to rest do so in peace. As an External Affairs Caretaker for Sleepy Hill, you will see to it that all deceased who leave the premises are returned to interment.

RESPONSIBILITIES
In this role you will:
- Maintain vigilance over "hot" areas of revival activity on the cemetery premises;
- Detect, pursue, corner, and neutralize those who wander away from Sleepy Hill;
- Comply fully with Centers for Disease Control and United States military guidelines for hazardous materials, blood-borne pathogens, viral and infectious outbreaks, and firearms safety;
- Assist law enforcement and national military

action when too many residents vacate the premises at once;

- Operate and maintain tactical equipment including but not limited to handguns, revolvers, semi-automatic rifles, shotguns, precision rifles, flamethrowers, chainsaws, tactical lights, holographic red dot and magnified optics, pole-arms, swords, knives, axes, clubs, and hammers;
- And other duties as unforeseen circumstances arise.

QUALIFICATIONS

- Previous experience or internship with military, law enforcement, funerary services, or, at minimum, certification in both basic and intermediate pistol and carbine courses.
- Hands-on experience with aggressive wildlife, including experience with tracking bipedal game animals.
- Certification in roadside medical assistance at the basic life support level or higher.
- Familiar with classical techniques for dispatching ambulatory deceased.
- A strong work ethic and an eye for detail.
- A strong cardiovascular system along with an athletic aptitude.
- A team player with exceptional marksmanship, swordsmanship, and critical thinking skills, and the ability to thrive in an interdependent or independent and stress-rich environment.
- Passionate about providing a restful afterlife, self-motivated, and eager to learn new skills and contribute to the success of the organization.

The ideal candidate would be strong, agile, a quick

thinker, have a cooperative mindset, and be skilled with a multitude of weaponry.

COMPENSATION:
Our employees at Sleepy Hill dedicate—and sometimes give—their lives to ensuring that those in the surrounding community rest as easy as those souls who stay entombed here.

We are committed to offering a compensation and benefits package that supports and rewards the contributions of employees on a "per capita" basis.

We work hard, but we also play hard! Our company hosts a variety of holiday functions on the premises, including a Halloween haunted house with "live" attractions.

We look forward to welcoming you to the Sleepy Hill team!

––––

Marcus Vance is currently moving, so will be living somewhere else when you read this. But he lives there with his wife, daughter, and dog. He is an Air Force veteran who writes speculative fiction and poetry. You can follow him on Twitter@MarcusCVance. Marcus has poetry and prose at Daily Science Fiction, Breath & Shadow, and Star*Line.

A story that stresses that you should follow all the rules when traveling.

Cemetery Hotel

Chris Barraza

The idea of booking a hotel next door to a cemetery in Kyoto thrilled Iris at first.

However, as she and the tour guide made their way through the dark moonlit labyrinthine plot of stone tombs jutting up from the earth like rows of sharp teeth, Iris came to regret that decision. They were in search of the headstone of one of the deceased. In her sweaty hands, Iris held a small package clumsily wrapped in a small piece of dark blue fabric printed with flowers and white rabbits that her friend Maura had given her earlier. Unlike Iris, she had no desire to venture into the graveyard, so she stayed behind in the safety of her hotel room.

Their tour guide, Togo, led the way. "When we get to the gravestone you'll place the item on top of the tomb. Then you will need to apologize for taking it in the first place." He turned to face Iris, then glanced at the bundle.

"Was it worth it?"

***

A few days earlier, as soon as the cab pulled up in

front of the Kyoto Court Arms, Iris leaped out and made a beeline for the cemetery next door. Just as promised, a large plot of land was filled with its own community of the dead. Vertical headstones in different lengths were lined up in rows in a patchwork of moist dirt, grass, and moss.

"Iris!" her friend Maura called out, while helping the cabbie lug their baggage from the trunk. "You forgot your things!"

Iris ran back to help, feeling slightly guilty. They had just graduated from the same college, and to celebrate a brief summer break before going out into the real world, they decided to treat themselves to a trip overseas.

Maura suggested Kyoto but Iris wasn't entirely sold on it. That was until Maura mentioned that Japan had its fair share of creepy stories and myths. Iris's guilty pleasure was spending hours on Reddit reading threads of scary stories.

The icing on the cake for Iris was when she found a reasonable hotel in Kyoto next to a cemetery. Maura had protested at first, but it was inexpensive, so she went along with it.

The ladies met up with Togo, who walked with them to their rooms on the fourth floor, explaining a few hotel rules and amenities.

"One more thing, ladies." Togo had been pleasant up until this point. He now spoke in a lower voice, practically whispering; his eyes boring into theirs.

"Do not take anything from this hotel. Toiletries will be provided in your rooms. It's OK to keep disposable toothbrushes and shaving razors. But no matter how nice, or cute, or interesting it may seem, never steal anything that isn't given to you. Do you understand?"

"Will we be billed for the missing items?" asked Iris.

Togo rubbed his temples and said in a harsh tone, "Promise me that neither of you will take anything!"

Both ladies reared back hearing him snap. Togo was hardly imposing with his salt-and-pepper hair and thick-rimmed glasses that reminded Iris of Garth in *Wayne's World*. But the break in character made them wonder if the whole pleasant tour guide business was just an act.

"Fine!" Iris responded, raising her hands in surrender. "We won't even keep the razors and toothbrushes!"

Togo stared at them, as if contemplating whether they were messing with him or being sincere. "See to it that you don't. For your sake." He grasped his luggage and headed to his room, reminding the pair that they had thirty minutes to settle in before meeting him in the lobby to go to lunch before touring the city.

When they arrived back at the hotel after dinner, Maura went to the rooftop *onsen* to soak her aching muscles. "I never thought temples and shrines had so many stairs!" she'd exclaimed.

Iris opted out when Maura reminded her that all bathers soaked nude. Instead, she found the nicest tea set on a shelf above the cramped minifridge in the narrow entryway of their room. The pot and teacups were ceramic, painted dark red and black, her favorite colors, with kanji characters engraved and painted over in gold. Iris knew a few characters, but she couldn't recognize the print on the cups.

Maybe that's why Togo told us not to rip off these

cups, she thought. *They probably say nasty things in Japanese to mess with tourists.*

She shrugged and began to make herself a cup of hot green tea from the complimentary bags next to the tea set. As soon as she drained her cup, she rinsed it out in the sink of their microscopic bathroom before wrapping it in a pair of clean socks and stashing it in her luggage. It was just one tiny cup, and what the hell, it was just too nice to pass up.

The next night, Iris decided to soak in the hot pool. When Maura had returned from the *onsen* the previous night she claimed that she felt like a new person. Even her skin seemed to be radiating with newfound energy. After a particularly brutal day hiking in the bamboo groves in Arashiyama, Iris decided to soak in the hot pool, nudity issues be damned.

The hot pools were on the top floor, one with a pink banner and the other with a blue banner over their respective doors. Iris entered the door with the pink banner, undressing in the locker room and rolling up her hotel key card inside her robe. She hesitated at the door leading to the pool before entering. Luck was on her side. The pool was deserted.

She gradually submerged herself in the near-scalding water, only stopping when the water gently lapped across her chest. The cement floor was a bit rough on her bottom, but she didn't mind as she closed her eyes when the ache in her legs ebbed away with the hot water. Iris could easily spend an eternity in the *onsen*.

She must have lost track of the time because the lights went out while she was soaking. She protested loudly, jumping to her feet in the water. The lights were still on in the locker room, casting a faint glow in the pool area. Suddenly, a cleaning lady stood in the doorway between the pool and locker room, blocking the scant light filtering inside.

"I'm still in here," Iris said. "Could you please turn the lights back on?"

The woman said nothing. She only glowered at Iris, her hands balling up into fists.

"Ma'am?" Iris couldn't figure out what was wrong with the cleaning lady. She had followed all of the pool rules, right?

The hotel cleaner slowly trudged toward the pool, stepping inside, still clad in her cotton pants and shirt. The water wrapped the cloth around her legs like a second skin.

"You know, I think I'll just get out now," Iris started climbing out, but a bestial roar erupted from the lady's mouth causing Iris to collapse back in the water, scraping her bottom on the rough cement of the pool floor.

The cleaning lady started laughing. Not so much laughing, but the guttural sounds coming from deep in her throat were a horrific parody of laughter, like a large animal trying to imitate a person. She trudged toward Iris, her garments falling from her body before her own flesh began to melt like wax, pooling into the water, exposing gleaming white bones underneath.

Iris could only gape at the skeleton leering at her. Somehow, she managed to jump out of the pool, ignoring the skeleton woman's claw-like fingers raking across her bare skin. Iris fled into the locker room, grabbing her robe before running out into the hallway. She struggled to put her robe on as she ran screaming down the hall. She ran smack into Togo, clad in his *yukata*, as he waited patiently for the elevator. Both of them fell to the floor, Iris screaming at the confused guide while he snapped back at her in Japanese.

"Calm down," he ordered, turning away from her. "And please, cover up!"

Iris wrapped her robe closed. She then sputtered about the cleaning lady who melted into a skeleton right before her eyes. Togo listened, frowning behind his thick-rimmed glasses at her.

"How much sake did you drink at dinner?" was all he said when she had finished.

"'How much sake'...what the fuck? I just saw a woman melt in there! And that's all you can say?" Iris sank to her knees, panting from exhaustion and disbelief.

Togo rubbed his neck as he looked at her. "I think you may have had a little too much to drink. Or . . . did you forget your promise?" He folded his arms across his chest. "You took something from the hotel, didn't you?"

Iris blushed with embarrassment and said, "Well, I wrapped up a teacup in my suitcase, but it is not officially stolen. It's still in the room."

Togo shook his head sadly and sighed. "I asked you not to take anything! You've upset the spirit of the original hotel owner."

It was well past midnight when Togo took Iris to the cemetery next door to deliver the stolen cup and apologize to the hotel owner's tombstone. She protested at first saying she would just leave the damn cup in the mini bar where she found it.

Togo shook his head at her. "You've angered his spirit. Even if you replace the cup, his ghost will continue to haunt you. That incident in the *onsen*? That was just a hint of what he has in store for you."

"I don't understand," Iris said. "Why is his spirit so angry with me for taking a teacup?"

"It's the principle of the matter." As they walked between the towering headstones jutting up from the moist ground like rows of jagged teeth, Togo told her about the original hotel owner, Takeshi. He was sitting alone in the dining area late one night when his hotel was robbed. The thief took the money from the cashier's desk, but also attacked Takeshi, demanding that he surrender his valuables. Despite handing over his wallet, the poor man was stabbed anyway and bled to death.

"Takeshi's family placed his ashes in this cemetery so he could remain close to the business he loved. But his spirit has no tolerance for thieves, and anyone stealing from the hotel will be punished from beyond the grave."

"This has happened before?" Iris queried.

Togo looked away, silent. She took the hint and continued following him like a scolded pup.

When they came to Takeshi's grave, Iris removed the teacup from a dark blue cloth Maura had handed her to protect it. Iris gently placed the teacup on the edge of the grave marker. She apologized to the tombstone before backing away, waiting for the spirit to arrive.

Takeshi's spirit emerged from behind his headstone, a near middle-aged man dressed conservatively in the same dark blue suit he'd worn the night he died. The jacket was ripped in several spots, oozing dark blood.

He plucked the teacup from the gravestone, looked at Iris and frowned.

"Togo? Why is he still angry?" Iris began backing away, bumping into the shivering guide.

"I don't know," he replied. He slowly approached the spirit, walking slightly hunched, trying to reason with it, but Takeshi lunged at them, yelling in Japanese.

"Run!" Togo stood upright, grabbing Iris's wrist, and they sprinted across the mossy ground. Iris looked back to see Takeshi chasing them, bellowing at them. She had no clue what he was saying, but seeing the ghost teeth exposed, globs of spittle flying out of the corners of his mouth, she knew he was out for blood.

Why is he still pissed? He got his cup back.

Togo had reached the edge of the cemetery before Iris, collapsing on the cement. He took a box of salt he'd bought at a convenience store earlier, making a circle around him, pausing only briefly to command Iris to hurry.

She didn't see the tree root jutting up from the soil as she dashed toward the tour guide. Iris tripped and fell, gritting her teeth in pain, and looked back at the ghost gaining on her. It began to alter its shape into a ghastly skeleton. Flat teeth sharpened into animal fangs as it continued to bellow.

Iris was frozen to the spot, too terrified to move.

"I'm sorry!" Iris cried. "What do you want from me?"

With an inhuman snarl the ghost pressed its bony face into hers. It grabbed Iris's shoulders, dragging her away from the edge of the graveyard. Iris cried out, her body scraping painfully along the hard dirt. She feebly tried pulling free, but the ghost had an iron grip. Togo shrank as the distance grew between them. Gathering up the last of her strength, Iris called out to him, "Help me!"

The man remained at the edge of the cemetery, obviously frozen with fear.

Iris managed to dig into her pockets, dropping some of her spare change and folded bills hoping the monster would accept her meager offerings. She pulled out Maura's blue cloth, noticing the tag on edge.

Property of Kyoto Arms Hotel.

The skeleton gave a hard yank, causing the cloth to flutter form Iris's sweaty hands. She screamed, desperately trying to grab the cloth, but the monster only quickened his pace, ignoring her pleas to look back at the blue fabric lying on the ground as he dragged her toward his grave.

———◆———

Chris Barraza resides in El Paso, Texas, land of eternal sun and tumbleweeds. She has always loved reading and began creating her own storybooks in elementary school. A love of creepy stories and guidance from a creative writing class in high school continued to influence a path in writing. When she isn't teaching American literature to high school students or traveling, Chris continues to pen stories into the wee hours, emerging from her writing for a reality check and iced coffee. She has written for the Canadian horror anthology Devolution Z. This is her second published work, and yes, she did explore a cemetery in Kyoto prior to writing this story.

A parent's love can be like wearing blinders.

Nineteen-Eighty-Something

Quinn Hernandez

You were in the process of drying up the last glass in the dish rack when you happened to look out the back window and noticed your son, Jacob, had left the spade still encrusted with dried dirt out by the burn pit. The mid-afternoon clouds threatened rain, and it was a pet peeve of yours when anyone left the garden tools out to get wet—the rust just ruined them—so you had to get it before disaster struck.

You put the last glass back in the cupboard, spread out the damp hand towel across the rack, then slipped on the old tennis shoes you kept around for gardening and mowing grass. There were five minutes to go until *Days of Our Lives* came on; should be plenty of time to get that shovel in the garage, and then you could relax and watch your shows until it was time to pick Jacob up from school.

But when you reached the burn pit and retrieved the

shovel, your curiosity got the better of you. What was he doing with the spade, anyhow? Jacob was not exactly the outdoorsy, adventurous type. In the past, it was like pulling teeth to get him out of his room to play outside. That was just how he was.

But that changed about a month ago, when Jacob started spending a lot of time down there, which, if he were an average child, it would not have been a big deal; but it was strange to you that your little hermit was now interested in the ravine out back. *Days of Our Lives* was going to have to wait. You had to see what was so interesting about these woods.

Jacob had worn a slight trail down the side of the ravine, which slopped at a forty-five-degree angle to the bank of a small creek. Then the woods leveled out and ran another thirty yards into the neighbors' property. You followed your son's path down to the bed of the creek. Once there, all around where you stood, you easily spotted about a dozen lumps of upturned earth, each about a foot in diameter. The weeds were thin here, so they stood out like a sore thumb. Most of the lumps were dried and hardened, all but one. This pile was three feet to your right, its soil was still dark, moist; it looked to be recently dug up. *Did he bury something?*

You used the shovel like a broom, swiping aside the loose earth. It didn't take long to find what he had buried. It looked to be the remains of a squirrel, or what was left of one. It looked to be fresh. Had it been torn apart by a dog? Why would he bury pieces of a squirrel?

You moved on to another mound. This one required a little more effort, but again, you didn't have to dig very far. This grave held the body of a bird, still in the process of decomposing; it even had some feathers still attached.

The next held another squirrel, another had a ground-hog. You stopped your digging. You had seen enough. You made your way back up the trail. You put the shovel back in the garage like you intended to do in the first place, then you took off your shoes and left them to the mudroom, then you head straight upstairs to Jacob's room.

The discovery of Jacob's graveyard hadn't really concerned you yet. Kids are naturally curious, so it wasn't exactly a new thing; children having a morbid curiosity. *But to bury them? Was this Jacob trying to do something decent by giving these poor things a proper burial?* You so wanted to think so. But in the back of your mind, in the pit of your stomach, you knew something was off.

So you stood before the foot of Jacob's bed, and you took your time, and you carefully scanned his room for anything out of the ordinary. But unlike the makeshift cemetery in the woods, this something was not easily detected. You were all but ready to give up your search and go downstairs to catch the last of *Days* when, at the last second, you noticed something unremarkable, but it caught your eye nonetheless.

Both your knees popped as you bent down to examine the cold-air vent. The screw on the left was missing; its twin was still there, but it had been untightened. There was a faint line—an arch—scratched into the paint, made by the corner of the vent. You tried it for yourself, and sure enough, the vent swiveled on the lone screw, the corner riding the mark. If you hadn't been suspicious you would have never noticed it. *Clever*, you thought, *but he is still only ten. He never thought to pull that corner out to prevent it from digging in.*

You squinted for a closer look inside. There was a blanket of thick dust resting on the flat, metal surface. The duct ran to the right about a foot, then dove down through the floor. In front of you, amongst the dust bunnies, was a large Ziploc bag. Even in the darkness of the vent you could make out what was inside it. You reached in, pulled it out, then turned to his bed and dumped out its contents. Twenty or so Polaroid photos fell like dead leaves upon his comforter. You quickly cast the bag aside and spread out the pictures.

A cold shock flashed through your stomach as your hand instinctively went to your gasping mouth; all of a sudden you feel nauseous.

You force a trembling hand to pick one up. In it, a groundhog had been split wide open; its innards had been scraped out and placed in a circle around the rodent; its head looked to be smashed in. The next photo showed a bird. It had a multitude of needles sticking out of it. The third picture you picked up was the worst. It was of a cat. Its limbs and tail were nailed to some sort of board, and the head was blurry, meaning it must have been moving when he took the picture. This last photo dropped from your hand to join the others.

What were these? Trophies? Something in you forced you to glance at them for a second time. Again, all you saw was death and mutilation and horror.

You collapsed on the floor and cried. *He was only ten years old. He was in the fourth grade, for Christ sakes! He liked to watch ALF; he played with his Transform-*

ers. *He was thoughtful, respectful, and he always did his chores without a complaint. Not to mention he got good grades and he helped his grandmother in her garden. Hell, thunderstorms made him nervous. So how was he capable of doing these . . . things?*

Then it hit you. Maybe there had been signs.

***

Jacob had always been a loner; he has no friends to speak of. When he was forced into social situations, he shut down and ignored everyone's attempt at interaction. Kids could be standing a foot away, talking directly at him, and he would not respond to them. He would just stare at the ground and wait for them to give up and go away.

Last year, your mother had bought him that Polaroid for Christmas, and the first picture he took was of a raccoon that had been run over in the street. You didn't think much of it then. You did ask him *why* he wanted a picture of it, but he just shrugged his shoulders. At the time, that was good enough for you.

The one thing that stuck out in your mind the most was the time when you were choking on a chunk of roast. It was just you and Jacob that night. The meat had gone down the wrong way and you just couldn't get it to come up. It may have only been a few seconds, but panic had started to set in. You absolutely could not breathe. The fear on your face had to be clear as day. Yet, when you looked to your loving son for help—just a pat on the back to help jar the chunk loose—all you saw was his stone-cold face. There was no concern in his eyes; he hadn't even moved. He just sat in his chair looking like a bored statue, watching you struggle.

And when you finally managed to cough up the meat, and you were able to regain your composure, you asked him why he hadn't helped. He again only answered you with a shrug and an emotionless stare.

Back in his room, you were still on your knees. Your eyes were puffy and red, your cheeks wet with tears. You wiped your nose with the back of your hand and tried to think of something to do. The word *monster* flashed through your mind. You had to tell someone. You had to get help. *But who? The police? What would they do? Would they want him committed? Maybe, arrest him? Call a shrink? Would he even talk to one?*

You sat in Jacob's room for hours, and thought about what should be done, what could be done, and also what *you* may have done wrong along the way.

You look over to the framed picture of the two of you sitting on his nightstand by the bed; you both looked so happy. That got you thinking about him when he was a baby. The details return: like the way his tiny mouth would snap open when you brought his baby spoon up to it; or the way he would laugh when you would blow raspberries into his belly; you recalled the moment he took his first step; when he first called you *mama*; or how he had reached out to you, crying, when he fell down, like the only thing in the world that was going to make it better was your hug.

***

You smile. No matter what happens, no matter how old he gets, he will always be that little baby to you.

You look at his clock. It tells you that you must be at Ridgewood in twenty minutes to pick him up.

Crypt Gnats

You finally get to your feet and take a couple of slow, deep breaths to help clear your head. You know full well what you must do.

First, you gather the photos and put them back in the Ziploc bag, and you take them to your room where you put them in the drawer of your nightstand. Then you head downstairs and put on your shoes and grab your keys. You take a last look at yourself in the mirror in the hall by the front door, and you try to rub the red out of your eyes and fix your hair the best you can with your fingers, and then take your leave.

Once you pick up Jacob, you will treat him to McDonald's, then you'll see if he feels like renting a movie for tonight. Of course, you will talk to him about the pictures— tomorrow; after you burn them. But for now, the thing you decide you both need tonight, is some good quite time alone. After all, this is just a phase. He is a still a good boy; he just made a mistake. To think how they would label him; how they would judge him. You have seen it on TV. Those men who killed. *They* were the monsters. *They* were those things society had no use for. Jacob is not like them. He is no monster. He is just a boy—*your* baby boy. And you would never let anything happen to him, ever.

So help you God.

———•———

Quinn is a family man and construction worker from the Midwest. His work can be found in the anthologies Fearology: Terrifying Tales of Phobias, Zombie! Zombie! Brain Bang!, D.O.A., Through the Eyes of the Undead and 100 Horrors to name a few. He thanks you for eading his bio.

Sometimes things aren't as they seem.

The House of Lonely Vines

Jennifer Lee Rossman

The house sprung up almost overnight in the field McKenna was not allowed to play in.

She never saw construction workers or heard a hammer strike a single nail, but every time she peered out from behind her curtains, it had grown a little more. First the foundation, leeching up from the charred land, then a ground floor with wraparound porch. Then a second story, brick by brick by brick, and finally a SOLD sign staked into the fresh, green lawn.

No one else in the foster home saw it happen, but then no one else liked to look at the cursed property that somehow still smelled of fire all those years later.

On their way home from school, children would dare each other to step over the property line. The braver ones would even close their eyes and stand with their backs to the overgrown field where the house and its family had burned alive.

Crypt Gnats

They never did find the body of the little girl. Some people said she had escaped unharmed, others said her bones had turned to ash and blown away, but there was one thing everyone agreed on: If you got close enough to the empty lot, you could still hear her screaming.

But the land didn't look cursed anymore. It looked like a home.

A lady appeared on the porch, beckoning to McKenna, who was looking out her bedroom window. In the time it took McKenna to slip outside, a husband had joined the woman, standing stiff and smiling as if posing for a family photo. His hand rested on the shoulder of a girl who wasn't there. A mother and father waiting for a daughter.

McKenna stood on the edge of the cursed land. The house called to her. A perfect home with a perfect family, just like she'd always wanted.

Only when she stepped over the property line did the house reveal its true self.

It was a crude carving of what a house should be, its gnarled roots spreading across the broken land. The porch railings jutted up like wooden splinters, gray and brittle. Scorch marks painted the brick walls like ghosts of the flames that had consumed it, and choking vines snaked through the bodies of the man and woman, roots erupting from their lifeless eyes as it held them upright like dolls.

McKenna tried to run, but it was too late. A thick vine curled around her ankles, dragging her up onto the porch where the roots began taking hold.

The lonely land, desperate for a family to love it, had grown the house from the ashes of broken dreams and its family from the remains of their bones and blood.

Crypt Gnats

They never did find the body of the little girl, for the house had found a suitable replacement.

And if you dare, get close enough to the empty lot that still smells of fire all these years later.

———•———

Jennifer Lee Rossman is an autistic and physically disabled sci-fi writer and editor. Her work has been featured in several anthologies, and she co-edited Love & Bubbles, a queer anthology of underwater romance. Her debut novel, Jack Jetstark's Intergalactic Freakshow, was published by World Weaver Press in 2018. She's been published in Cast of Wonders, Luna Station Quarterly, and Neon Druid. She blogs at jenniferleerossman. blogspot.com.

Grave robbing isn't always the safest vocation.

Mother Misery

Dorothy Davies

Now, is it my fault Marty decided to disinter the corpse?

I suppose it's my fault I went along with it, but what do you do when your best mate says they want help to dig up something of great value?

Well, you think, if he's that good a friend, he'll share the value with you. Right?

So there we were, eleven o'clock on a night fit to freeze your hanging bits clean off, with specially dulled spades so the moonlight didn't shine on the blade—he thought of everything, did Marty—shoveling—or should that be spading?—earth out of the grave of old Mother Misery.

Now you should know that wasn't and isn't her name. She was actually Mrs. Annabel Miller, but she was the picture of misery when she was alive, and I didn't suppose she would be much better looking now she was dead and cosmeticked and combed and powdered and all the things that the undertakers do to make you look good. What for? No, these were thoughts I could not speculate on as I sweated under my black waterproof with the effort of shifting the earth.

"What are we doing this for?" I muttered. Not a real question, you understand, just a . . . what are they called? Rhetoric or something question. But Marty answered for all that.

"She was buried with a gold chain round her neck, see, and hanging from it is a pendant, see, with markings on it which everyone says was the clue to her treasure, see, and I want it."

I gotta tell you, at this point I put down my spade and stared at my best friend who was still digging and sweating, and I swear he was shit scared, so he was. I wanted to know why. I didn't want to ask why. I hoped he would tell me by himself.

He didn't.

So I had to ask.

"What's got you scared, then, Marty?"

"Me? Scared? Nah, you got it wrong, old mate. I just don't like digging up the dead, is all."

"So, why are you?"

"I'm not. We are. Get digging."

So I dug.

And the spades went *clang* on the coffin lid and we both jumped like someone had spooked us.

And the moon went behind a cloud at that very moment and we were in total darkness. I swear Marty squeaked like a mouse, but I can't prove it and would never mention it to him anyway.

Now I'm not saying I was the big bold friend who never got scared 'cause that wouldn't be true, but I swear I wasn't as scared as him. I did hope he didn't notice the strange smell coming from my pants.

He carried right on working; I give him that. Scraping the earth off the coffin lid and making enough space for him to get down there and start unscrewing the lid. Well, he was no bigger than a whisper, so it was easy for him. I'm a bit . . . bigger than that.

The screws came out easy; but then, who would have thought, when they put them in, someone would be along to get them out again? He tugged and pulled, and then there she was. Mother Misery in all her rotting glory.

And there was the gold chain in all its shining glory, like it had just been cleaned.

And do you know he lifted that chain off over her head so delicate like I was shocked and moved. I truly was.

Before you could say Mother Misery no more than ten times, the lid was back on, the screws in place, Marty was out of the grave and we were demonically shoveling the earth back in. The moon came out again to help; I just hoped Marty thought the damp patch in front was a night shadow. Then I realized first, he had hisself the same damp patch, and second, I could smell the same smell from his pants as from mine, and knew he wouldn't dare say a word.

"Let's get outta here!"

I never heard more welcome words from anyone. We legged it out of that cemetery like we were training for the Olympics. At the street corner he banged my shoulder with his fist.

"See you tomorrow, mate. Thanks for that." And he was gone, racing for his home like demons were after him.

God, I thought we got out of the boneyard fast enough, but the speed he went was amazing.

I slunk indoors, ripped off the soiled pants, bundled them up and put them in a carrier bag to put in the rubbish, washed myself off, and crawled into bed. And spent the night remembering the look on the old girl's face when the lid came off.

She looked as if she was gloating.

Anyway, Marty come 'round the next night and we went down to the pub for a pint or three, and he pulled the chain and pendant out under cover of the dark corner we were in and showed it to me.

There were the markings all right, but hell, they could have been anything. Would have needed someone with specialist knowledge to decipher them. Marty said, "Got to go see a witch tomorrow, someone what knows about these things. She said she can read the signs."

"How much?"

"Doesn't matter, when we find the treasure . . ."

***

Now comes the strange bit, which I can tell you worried me more than a little.

Marty started losing weight. Like, loads of it. Like, he were no more than a whisper before, then he was all ghost. No body at all to speak of. No voice; he just about gave out a hiss. Had no money, spent it all on finding a witch who could read the signs and lead him to the treasure. Not a one of them could do it.

Marty stopped eating last week. They said it wouldn't be long before he was in his grave. He said he couldn't eat; it was choking him. He said he wished he'd never gotten hold of the damn chain and pendant. He offered it to me, and I refused it. He said I was sensible, and he wished he'd refused it.

I went to his funeral today. Would you believe that he was the next person to die after old Mother Misery, so he's buried right alongside her?

No wonder she was gloating. All she has to do is reach out through her box and he's right there, isn't he? The man who stole her pendant.

God alone knows what she'll do to him.

———◆———

Dorothy Davies has been a writer virtually all her (long) life, becoming a novelist just over thirty years ago. Twenty years ago she began editing professionally, which has given her a wide range of experience. She is a medium and publisher of a spiritual magazine, Circle of Light, which she edits. prepares, prints and dispatches herself. A one woman enterprise which has brought comfort to many. Her stories have appeared in a wide range of publications, including SF Trails and many Static Movement and other horror anthologies.

Getting lost in a mysterious forest can prove to be interesting

Whose Woods These Are

Colin Newton

The first thing that Gregory Chessman did was get himself completely lost.

He didn't know if that was the right thing to do, or if there was a right thing to do in this case. *They never prepare you for this kind of thing*, he thought. *Whoever they are.*

When in doubt, it was always safe to blame the weather. It had been unseasonably hot this winter. The entire situation could easily be pinned on that.

Here he was, building up a sweat, and it was the middle of the night. In January.

Of course, he was also pulling a couple of particularly heavy trash bags—the black kind, the kind for yard work—behind him. And a shovel.

"Getting myself lost," Gregory muttered before letting the phrase trail off. He then repeated it a few more times to himself. It was a mantra, a razor focus. "Getting myself lost," he said finally, "was intentional." It was a sobering consideration, and he stopped, the bags stopping with him. They all ground to a halt in the carpet of dead leaves, and Gregory was suddenly aware that the only sound he'd heard had been his own footsteps.

This was not who he was supposed to be. It was not in his character. Gregory Chessman was not the kind of man who got lost in the woods, dragging plastic trash bags and a shovel, well after midnight in January. Gregory Chessman was the kind of man who looked at his shoes when he talked to strangers. The kind of man who couldn't even stand to stare too long at his own reflection. And yet, here he was.

He started pulling the bags again but only for a second. His sobering sojourn into the subconscious had made him decide that, if he really was lost, and the road was nowhere to be seen, then this was as good a place as any. He released the bags from his grip, and their mouths drifted into the leaves. A pink hand tumbled out of one of the bags after it settled, as if the contents of the bag were trying to settle themselves too.

Gregory hefted the shovel up, and, despite his cold sweat, he started digging.

***

Before he got himself lost, before the unfortunate events of the weekend, before the unseasonably warm winter, the entire thing had started with Martin Rodale. Martin Rodale and Liz Chessman. Gregory's wife.

He wasn't entirely sure where they had first met Martin. Neither Gregory nor Liz moved through any extensive social circles. It must have been at an office party, or the house of a friend of a friend—his or his wife's, it didn't matter—where they had first met him. Gregory hadn't really thought too much of Martin at first, but by the time he had, he knew.

It was hard not to know, really. He could tell by looking at them why Liz preferred Martin. Martin was everything Gregory was not: healthy, hairy, of the earth. All of his features came to one sharp point, while Gregory's were lost in sad circles.

The affair started off innocently enough. They saw him at a party, went out for drinks once or twice, went out for dinner. There was nothing too suspicious about that. And yet, the nights out started to stack up, until Gregory realized he didn't know how much time Martin and Liz might be spending alone.

But as long as Gregory was there, he saw the way that they looked at each other. They seemed to speak to each other with a secret, shared language, like he had heard twins utilized, something that transcended words.

He had never meant for it to go this far.

That weekend, Gregory's wife was going to be miles outside of town at a company retreat. So, he called Martin and invited him over for dinner. "Just the three of us."

Later that day, Gregory called Martin again, and said that he was running late, that he had been ensnared at the office, that he wouldn't be home until well into the dinner hour, but Liz was expecting Martin and he shouldn't wait for him.

Of course, Gregory was sitting at home the entire time, and his wife was not. She was already far away from Wi-Fi and cell towers.

Martin did not arrive as fast as Gregory expected, but that just gave him more time to mentally prepare. He did something he rarely did. He thought back to his childhood, trying desperately to inhabit a body and brain that were now alien to him, the identity of little Gregory Chessman having long since been claimed by faded photographs and old drawings torn from refrigerator doors.

Gregory was not the kind of man who meditated on time, either its passage or its past, but he felt a touch of that significance now.

Indeed, when he looked at the clock, Gregory was surprised by how long it had taken Martin to show up. And he had to admit that Martin looked genuinely, innocently surprised when he did appear. But it would be hard to not look surprised when someone pointed a gun in your face.

Gregory had only intended to scare Martin with the gun. He had no idea the thing would go off. He'd never felt the need before to stare in mute wonder at a corpse he had created. He didn't want to drag a body into his bathtub so he could spend an hour cleaning up his wall. The whole thing was one of those acts of God. It just couldn't be his fault. But it was his problem.

How does one get rid of a body? he wondered. Telling the police was out of the question. He knew that it always was out of the question at times like these.

And Gregory also knew that if he was even remotely aware of where he got rid of Marin, he would crack. How could he deal if he knew where the thing was?

The woods of Pan's Glen seemed like an appropriate place to do it. The area, set aside by the Forest Service for preservation, was labyrinthine and eternally autumnal, and it lent itself well to local legends of eerie presences, shadowy figures in the distance and unsubstantiated disappearances. It was also an hour's drive from town, and Gregory had only been there twice, neither time being all that fun. It was exactly the kind of place for him to lose himself.

The warm weather meant the ground wasn't frozen over, and the digging didn't seem to take that long. At least, not compared to cleaning his wall. Nothing could possibly seem long after that. When it was done—when all of it was done—and he was walking back to his car, Gregory realized he really hadn't taken a look at the forest while he'd been dragging the bags. That had been the point, of course, not knowing where he was. But it also meant he hadn't considered the getting back part.

He glanced up. The branches of the trees wrapped around the sky with arthritic talons. There was no moon. He couldn't remember if he'd seen moonlight earlier. He was almost certain he had, but he barely paid attention to the moon. Why would he? Either way, it hardly mattered now. Whether he was remembering wrong, or whether the teeth of the trees had gobbled whatever did hang in the sky, there was nothing to see now. Even a discernible wind could have given him a sense of direction, but it was barely present, only heard in the form of a distant and vaguely melodic piping sound. It didn't help that Gregory felt as if he was being watched. A natural reaction, he supposed, given what he had just done, but he hadn't felt like he was being watched when he was going into the woods. He picked up his pace.

After a few minutes punctuated only by his footfalls,

Gregory mumbled, "These woods are infuriating. There's no sense of . . ." He let it die. *Direction*, he finished in his head.

Keeping his steady pace, he felt that the tree line had gotten thicker. Not just that, the trees blurred into mirror images, two single-file lines, two fat trees stretching backwards into Eden and forward toward infinity, with no sign of the moon and no sign of his car.

The local legends were coming back to him. It wasn't Bigfoot or alien abductions. It was devil worshipers, or rumors of others who used the primeval forest to conjure up horned figures with sacrificial rites. Their rites were described in vague whispers that invoked cold nights and hot blood every time someone disappeared or the Forest Service closed off a section of the Glen. It was easy to call it gossip around a single-serve coffee maker and under florescent lights. It was difficult in darkness. Every unseen rustle became the movement of a cloaked figure; every blurred outline became a harsh face; and there it was again, the feeling that he was being watched. Gregory wasn't sweating anymore; the sweat had frozen on his forehead. He suddenly felt very glad he was holding the shovel. He pulled it close to his chest and started to run.

In a few minutes, he realized that the trees didn't look like a blur because they had actually grown closer together; they looked like a blur because someone was running beside him, matching him step for step, blending the tree line into a single, continuous march, like a constantly changing figure on a roll of speeding film. Except when he looked to his right and his left, the someone was there, simultaneously in both places. He stopped, and the forest stopped with him. Everything was quiet.

Then the forest rose up in front of him—not the forest, but a figure, covered in dead winter leaves like a fur coat, arms and grasping hands raised in silent praise to the trees. Gregory surprised himself when he swung his shovel, like a tennis player straining for a ball, and struck the figure in what he instinctively hoped was its head. The shovel connected with a fat slap. There was an ear stretching scream, like something being boiled alive, and the figure tumbled to the ground.

Without waiting to see if it rose, if it was still capable of rising, Gregory swung his shovel again and again against the figure's head. Whether he tired of swinging first or the figure stopped squirming, Gregory couldn't say. All he knew was that after what felt like an eternity, the hard tissue gave way with a squelch, and Gregory sank to the ground, breathing heavily.

After his breathing steadied, he stood up and looked down. Cautiously probing it with the shovel, Gregory used his foot to push away some of the leaves.

Whatever it was, it was not human. It was shaped like a man, but it was easily a foot taller than Gregory and far more robust. Its skin was gray or brown—it was hard to say in the dark—with a hoary, knotted musculature beneath. Rough looking patches of sparse hair graced its shoulders and chest.

But it was the head. Despite a deep, sagging crack that was oozing thick bile, it was clearly a goat's head. It had a broad, flat nose, cruel slits for eyes set far from the middle, and an impressive pair of curved horns that looked like ornamental carved tree branches jutting from its temples.

Gregory was motionless for a long time. The tree line looked sparser than it had a few minutes ago, and moonlight returned and spilled through the ancient branches. But he still had no idea where he was.

Gregory shook his head, propped the shovel on his shoulder, grabbed one of the thing's horns, and with some difficulty began pulling it through the leaves. *I've already buried one body tonight*, he thought to himself. *How long can it take to bury another?*

———◆———

Colin Newton is a Los Angeles based freelance writer. He blogs about movies, monsters and metaphysics at Idol-sAndRealities.wordpress.com. *This is his first fiction published in an anthology.*

Perfect is definitely in the eye of the beholder.

Perfection

Adjusting the bow tie yet again, he studies himself. His reflection glares back: handsome as ever, admittedly, but not quite perfect. He grits his teeth, unties it for the third time to start again.

The knot finally arranged to satisfaction, he searches his mirror image for flaws. Flaws that might belie his noble blood, flaws that might give others the impression that he is—has been, since birth—anything other than their superior. The gentleman third in line for the Earldom of Radleigh should . . . no, *must* be flawless. Not a single dark blond hair out of place, ice blue eyes cool and commanding as ever, his suit impeccably cut, but still, something is missing . . . .

Ah!

He strides to the nightstand to tug a rose from the paper-wrapped bouquet atop the silly heart-shaped box of chocolates, suddenly so fashionable, for which he'd paid a small fortune. As the flower pulls free, three petals drift to the floor. With a muttered curse, he grinds them into the carpet with the heel of his shoe. He'd only bought the ridiculous blooms a few hours ago and had been assured by the malnourished and frankly odoriferous urchin selling them that they were fresh.

Of course the flowers are wilting. He wants . . . no, needs everything to be perfect tonight. Thus, everything that can go wrong, will.

Forcing a deep breath, he attempts to compose himself. Flowers in February are bloody expensive to come by. Fanny had better damn well appreciate what she's given!

He catches himself. "Now, don't think like that, man. You're getting agitated over nothing. Everything will go splendidly."

Now then . . . why had he retrieved the blossom in the first place? Ah, yes.

He withdraws the penknife from his pocket and reaches for the rose a second time, then lets out a sharp yelp and drops it to examine his thumb where a crimson bead has begun to well up.

"Damn it to hell!"

He only just manages to stop himself from hurling the damnable rose, the bouquet, and everything else within reach into the fireplace.

Why, oh why do these things always happen to him? His life should be a lark! Instead it's one catastrophe after another without fail. It isn't right, and it isn't fair.

And yet, he remains resilient. First and foremost, a gentleman, through and through. He would exercise his good breeding and make the best of things, as he always does. No one can claim *he* isn't stoic. As his father, Lord Dumphrey, likes to say, "An upper lip so stiff, one would think it had been starched by the maid!"

A sharp exhalation as he gathers himself for yet another attempt. This time, he manages to trim the stem and place the rose into the jacket buttonhole without further injury or insult. Adjusting it in the mirror, his eye falls on the dark smear that now stains one of the petals. He reaches for a handkerchief to wipe away the blood, then stops; it will make an amusing story to recount later to Fanny. He can tell her all about the trials and tribulations he'd had to endure just to hand her a bouquet of roses on Valentine's Day.

Maybe she'll actually appreciate them for once. It's high time the spoilt girl realizes how lucky she is.

He checks his pocket watch; wouldn't want to be late. Examining his reflection one last time, he smooths his hair before gathering the gifts. Downstairs, he places them carefully on the hall table to bundle himself into his overcoat but, in his haste, his sleeve catches the bouquet, sending it the floor with a rustle.

Will his ordeals never end? By the time he delivers them into Fanny's grasping hands, the flowers will be un-recognizable, a bruised bunch of vegetable matter.

Ready at last, he steps into the night and is met by a wall of air so frigid that his lungs sting in his chest, com-plaining with every inhalation. He rejects the half-enter-tained notion of walking to their rendezvous; it won't do to arrive half-frozen, miserable and shivering. Clouds of breathy condensation hang about his head like pipe smoke as he hails a passing hansom.

Already shivering, he climbs inside the cab before he has even finished calling out the address; the driver, ap-parently sensing his hurry, clucks to the horse and the hansom jolts forward, throwing him off balance. He flings out an arm as he's thrown against the chill leather seats. When he manages to settle himself, he realizes—*sure enough*—that the hapless bouquet has been crushed beyond recognition.

He considers simply throwing the cursed thing out the window, shouting obscenities at the driver as he does so, but clenches his jaw. Deserved or not, such behavior is unbefitting of a gentleman of his stature. He'll simply short the driver on his fare. Someone needs to teach these people to respect their betters. Besides, it's not like the man would dare to say anything to him.

Instead of giving in to his temper, he removes the ribbon from the candy box and helps himself. After the night he's had, Fanny and her inevitable pouting can go to hell for all he cares. The chocolate is gone all too quickly, so he selects another with fingers stiff from the cold because, of course, he's forgotten his gloves!

He'd been so set on making this Valentine's Day perfect after the disaster that was last year's celebration. What a disappointment that had been.

He'd arrived on time, punctual as always, ready to enjoy a romantic dinner with his beautiful fiancée, but when she'd answered her door, it was clear something wasn't right. Her face, though striking as ever, had been an unhealthy shade of pale gray, lines creasing the normally flawless porcelain of her forehead. She'd still been lovely, of course: warm, honey brown hair falling in waves to her shoulders, lips plump and inviting, but now those lips were pursed in agitation, and her dark eyes flashed with worry when they landed on him.

The cab shudders to a halt, interrupting his reminiscences. *Here already?* He collects the pitiful remnants of his gifts and steps from the hansom. Digging into his pocket, he withdraws a few coins, which he hands up to driver. The man studies the scant amount and opens his mouth to say something, then glances at him and seems to think better of it. Muttering to himself, the driver clucks to the horse and pulls away.

At least the frigid February air lends itself to a crisp clarity. The moon brightly illuminating the path, he makes his way to the wrought iron gates—fortunately unlocked, one small bit of good luck in an otherwise hapless night. After a few paces, he veers right and steps onto the grass, brittle under his feet. Everything is frozen solid but, thank God, there's no snow to wet his trouser legs, no mud to ruin his shoes.

Perhaps the evening might just turn out all right after all.

His brow furrows as he cannot keep his thoughts from returning yet again to last year's fiasco.

Fanny's face when she'd answered the door and seen it was him.

The way she'd kept him on the stoop, that wary look in her eyes. He'd hated to see her marring her good looks with such an unflattering expression.

"Wh . . . what are you doing here?" she'd asked, her voice trembling.

He'd laughed at first. "Why, darling, am I that early? Are you not ready yet? Silly girl."

His incorrigible Fanny. Sometimes it truly annoyed him, how disorganized and forgetful she could be, but he'd shrugged it off, tried his best to find it endearing. Even now, he recalled pausing to mentally congratulate himself on that; it had always been one of his best traits, his patience with the less adept, his willingness to see the best in those not as gifted as himself.

"No, I . . . you . . . we talked about this . . ." she'd begun, but, growing bored, he had pushed past her and gone inside.

She'd turned in alarm, but he'd tried to soothe away her silly protests.

"Don't worry, darling, it's all right if everything isn't quite ready," he'd reassured her. "I *am* your fiancé, after all." Chuckling, he'd reached past her to shut the door that she had, in her habitual carelessness, left open. As he'd done so, his hand had brushed against her hair. She'd flinched.

At that, he had no longer been unable to stifle his irritation. "Come now, Fanny, what *is* the matter? You're skittish as a filly and it's downright idiotic, is what it is."

She'd set her jaw at that, visibly steeling herself. She might be infuriating, but it was adorable when she tried to exercise her will.

"No."

"Excuse me?"

He'd moved toward her, and she'd retreated until her back was against the wall. Her voice trembled a little, but she'd raised her chin. "No, we talked about this. I—"

"What, that ridiculous little argument? Is that what you've got yourself all upset over? Still?" He'd forced himself to suppress an eye roll, tried to inject some affection into his voice. "Oh, darling, it meant nothing. Don't worry your pretty little head another minute. I wouldn't want my future wife to get frown lines."

"No," she'd tried again. "I meant everything I said. I'm *not* your fiancée. You have to stop calling me that. I never was. I don't want to see you again. I tried to tell you. You're . . ." She drew a deep breath, closed her eyes. "Your temper, your impatience, your . . . You're cruel. You frighten me. I thought I'd made that clear last time."

He'd opened his mouth to reply, but she'd taken a quavering breath and, in a flurry, finished. "I want you to leave and not come back. Please. And if you don't, I'll . . . I'll be forced to inform the police."

His face had felt suddenly hot and cold at the same time.

How dare she. After everything he'd given her. The little tramp. She ought to be flattered and . . . .

And then he'd realized she was making excuses. Oh yes, there was someone else. Of course there was; that was the only explanation. Duplicitous little whore. His father had always tried to warn him: blood will out.

Before he could stop himself—but, why would he? Why should he have stopped himself? Even now, he found no fault in his actions. She'd needed to be taught a lesson. His arm had whipped out on its own accord to slap her across her lying face.

Open-handed though it was, he'd hit her harder than he'd intended. Of course he had; a gentleman never means to *injure* a woman, lady or, in her case, not. He'd simply reacted instinctively.

The dull thud of her body as it bounced off the wall had sounded surprisingly loud in the silence that followed the blow. She'd fallen to her knees, hand to the side of her face. The quiet continued, stretching on for seconds.

Then: Chaos.

Her single shocked gasp turned to loud sobs as she'd scrambled to her feet and rushed for the door.

Before she could reach it, though, his strong fingers had closed around her upper arm, whipping her about to face him. She'd instantly turned into a senseless animal, a feral little cat, all nails and teeth and thrashing limbs. Her incoherent screams drowned out his attempts to calm her and he'd reached up to take her by the shoulders, just to shake some sense into her. Instead, her shrieks had grown higher in pitch and volume, louder and louder; she wouldn't stop. He'd just wanted her screaming to stop. Stupid, hysterical woman! If she'd just stop screaming and listen! If she'd only shut up! It was just to get her to stop screaming, truly it was. Once she'd ceased that infernal racket, they'd be able to talk like sensible, refined—at least, on his part—adults.

If she would shut up.

If he could just get her to shut up for thirty seconds, so he could reason with her. So he'd moved his hands up and squeezed, just a little, as a warning, just until she'd stopped screaming. Then, when she didn't stop, just a bit harder. Then harder still. That slender throat of hers was so soft, it was barely any pressure, truly, it was just to make the noise end. He'd squeezed until finally, finally, the screaming had ceased.

With a sigh of relief at the blessed quiet, he'd loosened his grip to rub the bridge of his nose and gather his thoughts. When she'd collapsed, he'd rolled his eyes at this newest bout of theatrics.

His voice was unsympathetic. "Come now, Fanny, I've

had enough of your games. Let's stop this inanity, shall we?"

At her refusal to cooperate, to stand or even acknowledge him, he'd felt a flicker of rage returning. He'd bent down and grabbed a handful of her hair, raising her head to force the petulant creature to look him full in the face so that she could see his disappointment at her childish antics. Instead, his gaze had been met with unblinking eyes, spider–webbed with the red of burst vessels.

Now, walking to her for their date he shudders, from the cold but more from what had followed. The arranging and rearranging, the straightening and tidying, the breaking and messing all over again and then hailing a constable. Oh, the vulgarity of it all. He remembers the side-eyed looks from the squat constable, the nerve that such a low bred boor would *dare* doubt the word of Lord Dumphrey's heir! There was the futile search for the filthy, drunken beggar who had, in crazed desperation, committed the heinous act. He'd shown how the door had been broken in, how he had discovered his darling fiancée, her poor broken body, stripped and robbed. And of course there had been the final well-placed word from his father.

His thoughts return to the present and he reaches his destination, tutting at the bad memories. He traces his finger over the engraved letters.

FANNY WHITE

b. 1888 — d. 1907

Helping himself to another chocolate, he swallows before addressing the headstone. "Here I am, right on time, as always. Happy Valentine's Day, I've brought roses, see?

In fact, I've a funny story to tell you about these blasted flowers. You'll laugh when you hear . . . well . . . You won't interrupt, anyway. Tonight is going to be perfect."

———

After 5+ years of being a librarian in a small town in Western Maryland, Moira Gillen quit to pursue her dream of writing full-time. In addition to being a wife and mother, and writing shorter pieces (mostly dark fiction, horror, and speculative fiction), Moira is hard at work on revising her first novel manuscript, a ghost story entitled "Worm." Some of her more recent publications include the short story, "The Silence of Aeolian Hall," in Unnerving Magazine's gothic anthology "Haunted Are These Houses," as well a zombie short, "Amy," in Weird Mask Zine. One of her sci-fi pieces, "Crashlanding," was featured on the short story podcast "600 Second Saga."

Memories can certainly brighten the present.

Old Magic

John Kujawski

I thought of her evil grin as I dug my shovel into the dirt. It was a grin that I had always loved. Of course, Jessica always put a smile on my face as well. More than anything, I wanted our old magic back. I just needed something to give her as a symbol of what we had shared together in the past. My whole plan required that I head to the woods in the middle of the night. Luckily, I knew exactly where to go.

It had not been long since I had been through those woods in Missouri that I had always loved. I never understood how Jessica could leave and move to another state where I knew the woods were inferior to what we had in our home state. I thought of her as I walked to my destination in the late hours, remembering all the things we did together.

I was happy when I heard she was back in town. We had always enjoyed our evening activities. We would often laugh about the screaming and the occasional, necessary fights that we were involved in. After all, some people were the type who had a lot of spark in them. Jessica seemed to enjoy it all, often putting her hands through her red hair and giggling to herself. I always took pleasure in her happiness.

The thing about Jessica was that she was clever. I suppose I could be mysterious at times and no one thought there would be any trouble out of me in life. I was always a skinny guy who stayed fairly quiet. Jessica took things to the next level, though. I think people thought she was a girl who could do no wrong. Everyone I knew seemed to look at her as if she was the one good person in the room at any given time.

As far as nowadays, when it came to finding a gift for Jessica to relive the memories, I was just glad I still had my shovel.

As I kept digging into the dirt, I could feel the excitement building up in myself. I knew there had to be something special in the ground just waiting for me to take it. I wasn't as strong as I used to be, but I kept working it, tossing dirt into the air like I was still a pro. Finally, before I knew it, it appeared.

I pulled it out of the ground and held it up close. It was a joy just to see it with my own two eyes and I could feel those crazy feelings in my heart that I used to have when I was with Jessica. It was indeed the perfect item. I couldn't wait to take it home. I couldn't wait to put in a box for Jessica.

It had been so long since I held a human skull in my hand. There was nothing quite like my days with Jessica. We'd always seemed to find new people to kill.

———◆———

John Kujawski has interests that range from guitars

to the Incredible Hulk. He was born and raised in St. Louis, Missouri and still lives there to this day. He has been published in Rocking Horse Press, Far Horizons Press, and Forgotten Tomb Press

A dare and a cemetery at night are not a good combination.

The Thing in the Graveyard

David Odle

Nathan gazed across the dark cemetery and swallowed a lump in his throat. Shadowed gravestones dotted the vast expanse, some leaning heavily in the soft earth like dying soldiers.

I don't wanna do this.

"What's a matter, baby? Ya chicken shit?" Herby McIntire cackled. A few others laughed with him. "Ya scared the boogeyman's gonna grab ya and eat ya?"

Assholes. Nathan squeezed his hands into fists. Man, he'd love to bash Herby's fat face. "I ain't chicken," Nathan said. He was actually as chicken as chickenshit comes, but there was no way he'd let Herby see that. No way in hell.

Nathan's older brother, Dave, stood next to Herby with his hands shoved in his pockets. Nathan glanced at him . . . *a little help here?* Dave just stared uncomfortably down at his shoes.

"So, ya gonna do it, then?" Herby grinned showing too much teeth.

"Yeah," Nathan said, "I'm doin' it."

Strolling across an old cemetery at midnight wasn't exactly the epitome of courage, but it *was* scary. And if this is what it took to prove he wasn't chicken, then bring it on. *It's only half a mile, and I've walked it a million times.*

But never at night.

And the Black Rock Graveyard was haunted. Dave and his buddies had told him horrible stories one night with flashlights held under their chins, distorting their faces. *The boogeyman lives in there. . .*

Nathan shuffled onto the grassy edge of the cemetery and scraped his tongue across dry lips. The other boys remained on the road. Herby clapped and said, "Hey now, I do believe the baby's gonna do it."

"You guys'll be waiting for me, right?" Nathan wiped his sweaty palms against his jeans.

"You know it," Herby smiled, but the gesture never touched his eyes. "Swear to God. We're takin' the road and meetin' ya on the other side."

Nathan shot a look at Dave who nodded, and Nathan knew Dave wasn't bullshitting; Dave would be there.

He turned and stared straight ahead at the route he planned to take. A flood lamp cast dim light across freshly mowed grass, and Nathan knew that covering the first hundred yards or so wouldn't be a problem. He could sprint that. It was the deeper bowels of the graveyard that terrified him. In that place where the light couldn't reach and the blackness grew wicked and thick. *Just half a mile*, he told himself, *half a mile*. He'd ran a whole mile about two months ago, just before completing seventh grade gym class, and it took him ten minutes and thirty-two seconds. *You're fast for your age*, the gym coach had said and patted him on the shoulder. *You should run track.*

This was only half of that, but he also knew he'd have to walk some of it since it would be too dark to see, so he was looking at seven or eight minutes, max . . . .

I'm fast for my age. Seven or eight minutes of terror to shed the baby image. A steep price indeed, but one worth paying.

Nathan stole a final glance at Dave's solemn face and said, "You fuckers better be there."

And then he ran.

The cemetery ground had an incline at the front edge, a deceiving terrain feature at night. He stumbled, recovered, and charged forward. His feet beat thumps against the dewy grass, and he became aware of how loud his breathing was. Tree branches stretched down like skeletal fingers, reaching for his eyes as he whipped past, and the farther he ran, the more the light faded.

Half a mile . . . that's all.

Less than that now.

He slowed to a cautious walk for fear he might crash into something. He clenched his fists. The darkness swelled. As his dad would have said, it's blacker than a coal miner's ass out here.

Gravestone silhouettes loomed like gray ghosts and he swore something moved. His heart slammed and he wondered if he'd made it halfway across yet. Surely he was halfway. But ahead, only a black void greeted him, and he whimpered. Something horrid was out here, watching him, ready to pounce at any second.

The boogeyman.

Ya scared the boogeyman's gonna grab ya and eat ya?

Turn back! But which way was back? Holy God, he wasn't even sure if he was going the right way to start with!

The stench of wet earth festered in the air and the night grew thick. He kept moving, placing one foot in front of the other. Cold tears slid down his cheeks and he pictured his dad out here. He knew his dad wouldn't be scared. Not at all, and Nathan longed desperately to be like his dad.

That's when he heard it.

A twig snapped off to his left. It was something big. Nathan stopped, heart thudding, and tried to listen over his own breath. Another snap of a twig followed by a short rustle of dead leaves. *Oh Jesus . . .* His heart pounded so hard that his eyeballs throbbed.

"Herby?" his voice warbled. If one of those pricks was trying to scare him, he was kicking somebody's ass. But, oh God, how he hoped it was them.

No one answered.

His mind whispered, *You could be across by now if you weren't just standing here.*

The air, stagnate and dank, contained another smell; a rancid stink that he recognized. One he'd caught the whiff of many times while driving down the road with his dad. "Whew," dad would say, "you smell that? Somethin's dead out here."

Somethin's dead.

The stench wafted through the dark so awful that he gagged. It was as if the rot were alive and settling on his tongue. He retched again and nearly puked. What in the world was that?

Another rustle of leaves, then a heavy thump against the ground, followed by another. Something walking. Getting louder. And that smell. Oh God . . .

Somethin's dead out there, boy.

He peered into the dark, trying to catch a glimpse of whatever it was. *Run . . . run like crazy!* But he couldn't get enough air, like the blackness had sucked it all up.

A moan drifted out of the dark like tidal breath over dead vocal cords. He screamed right then. He screamed as that moan grew closer.

He was frozen until he heard the faint laughing. Barely heard it. Strange and distant, almost dreamlike, the far-off sound drifted through the darkness. *That's Herby laughing.* Somewhere out on the road, those guys were waiting on him, telling jokes amongst themselves, no idea he was hearing them. Holy shit, he was close!

Nathan wiped sweat from his forehead and stumbled backward, almost falling on his butt. *Run, you idiot,* and his feet finally woke up and moved. Whether he was running in the right direction, he didn't know, but by God, he was running somewhere. As long as it was away from that awful death smell.

He cried out with each loping stride. He wanted his mom and he decided right then that it would be OK to be a chickenshit the rest of his life. Herby McIntire suddenly seemed very irrelevant in the scheme of things.

That horrid moaning roared behind him. Chasing him. He sprinted harder. He couldn't tell if it was gaining, but he thought it might be, and if he tripped and fell, or ran into something . . . .

Then he saw it. Straight ahead, the black silhouette

lumbering across the graveyard toward him. Nothing he knew should be out here. A monster on two legs.

The boogeyman.

Nathan veered off to the right. If he slowed or changed direction it would catch him.

He raced with everything he had. The monster lurched shockingly fast.

"Boy!" It growled. "C'mere, boy!"

Nathan cried as he ran. That moaning behind him was just over his shoulder and he anticipated the grasp of cold hands onto his neck. There was no escaping it. The darkness was closing in, a blanket of nothingness, an inescapable abyss.

Suddenly the ground dropped out from under his feet and for a bizarre moment, he floated. The air stilled just before he collided with the road.

His ankle snapped as soon as he hit, then his knee smashed into rough asphalt. He sprawled onto his belly and slid when his chin cracked the surface and split it open, shattering two teeth.

He lay there a moment, knowing he was hurt, and waited for the cold, dead hands to descend on him.

But it was his big brother Dave's voice that caught his ears first.

"Holy shit, man!" Dave gasped.

Then Herby said, "What the hell happened?"

No one was laughing.

Dave's strong hands gripped his arm. Nathan tried to tell them that something was chasing him, but he couldn't speak. His mouth was full of something bitter, and thick. He blinked as Herby's face loomed over him. "Wow, man,"

Herby said, "he looks hurt."

"Help him up," Dave slipped his hands under him.

Nathan's eyes blurred and he must have passed out, because that's all he remembered until he woke up in the hospital. His mom held him as he cried, and his dad just stared at him thoughtfully from the edge of the bed. He told them all what had happened, about that thing chasing him. Of course, no one believed that part, and Dave got in some deep shit for allowing this all to happen.

***

From then on, he avoided Black Rock Cemetery; even in the daytime. Dave never spoke of it again. Neither did Nathan. And though the memory of that night faded, the nightmares never did. Even a decade later, Nathan still screamed himself awake; his body slick with sweat, the image of the monster lumbering after him still fresh in the dark.

And sometimes, on the worst nights, the monster would catch him.

———◆———

David discovered his love for writing at the age of twelve while growing up in Warren County, Indiana. He craves a great story and is blessed with a passion for creation. After seven years in the military and over thirteen years as an IT consultant, he now resides right back in Indiana with his wife and five children. His debut novel, Markus, is scheduled for release in 2019. If you'd like to follow David, visit his website at www.davidodle.com and subscribe to his email list. He would love to have you along! David published under the pen-name D. Leroy in StrangeFictions 'and in the Pop Machine anthology published by The Inwood Indiana Press

*A tale of greed, widespread betrayal and
retribution.*

Who Owns the Earth? Who Sells the Sky?

Andrew Punzo

"I don't even know why they got us ridin' in pairs anyhow. Greenie like you can't do much other than blabber,
'parently," Horsten said.

"Well . . . you heard what they've been sayin' at camp,"
McCloskey explained.

"Bull on that."

McCloskey's thin, wheedling voice piped up in protest. "But even some loggers have dis—"

"I said *bull*," Horsten barked.

McCloskey slouched in his seat, brow-length orange
hair protruding from his woolen watch cap over a narrow,
pale face.

Pops and misfires from the truck's laboring engine
punctuated the silence of the cold spring morning as it
trundled along the woodland road. After a while Horsten
began to feel sorry for him.

"Forgot your name."

"McCloskey."

"How'd the first day of loggin' go?"

McCloskey closed his eyes as if he were about to vomit. "Terrible. I was almost stabbed for lookin' at someone the wrong way, and I wasn't even lookin' at the fella!"

Horsten began a deep, rumbling laugh that halted when he saw the sick expression spread on McCloskey's face. "Takes a bit gettin' used to the camps, but once you ain't so green 'taint so bad."

McCloskey did not look reassured. "Other than loggin' there's no jobs out here for a fella like me. Nobody wants to hire Irish."

Horsten bit down on another laugh.

"But once we get this pulpwood to Bangor I'm callin' it quits with loggin'." McCloskey harrumphed and crossed his arms. "I like history. Did you know I almost went to secondary school?"

"No need for schoolin' out here," Horsten said with a mocking grin, exposing a gold-plated incisor.

"Well I was this close." McCloskey pinched his thumb and forefinger. "I was even readin' at camp about Bangor."

Explains why you almost got stabbed, Horsten thought.

"Did you know about the Indians that lived around here? For thousands of years?"

Horsten shrugged.

"They did. The Penobscot tribe. Until about the 1830s or so. Never had a problem with the lumber partnerships usin' the land either." McCloskey turned to look outside the window. "Then one day the mayor meets with the lumber barons and they draw up this treaty for loggin' rights on Penobscot land. But at the powwow, the chief says he wouldn't sign. Told the whole lot of 'em, 'Who owns the earth? Who sells the sky?'; he wouldn't budge!"

Horsten didn't respond. He drew his knife to cut a plug of tobacco with one hand while the other whitened around the knuckles on the steering wheel.

"So they cut the Indians down where they stood! Left them to rot where they fell. Even crucified the chief and stuffed a bunch of money in his mouth. Don't seem right though, don't it? I mean how can you—"

"Let me tell you how you can," Horsten growled. "Ain't nothin' matters out here but this n' this only." He reached into the breast pocket of his flannel jacket and pulled out a wad of bills that he smacked against McCloskey's forehead as if to deposit the notion into his brain. "This ain't women's work. You keep your head down n' do it. Ain't no other reason to be out here. You gettin' that same blood money, ain't cha?"

McCloskey's eyes darted to his own breast pocket.

"Ayuh. So you ain't no newborn baby Christ neither. Now keep your eyes peeled n' quit jawin' 'til Bangor." Horsten returned the bills and spat between his boots. "Problem with you is you got your head in the sky. Lookin' up don't matter. S'posed to be grounded, head down."

A half mile later he bore left at a fork in the road.

McCloskey coughed to break the tense silence. "Was that the right way?"

"Hellfire! 'Course it was! I've been loggin' for years, I know my way 'round these woods better n' any of your Injuns would've."

"I don't remember that split."

"Well . . . well we can't turn around until we hit a wider cut, so's no choice but to keep goin'."

McCloskey softly spoke again after another mile. "I don't recognize any of this."

"How could ya? It's all green, ain't it?"

Now McCloskey was the one who sounded disinterested. "Yes, but these are oaks. Hardwood trees. Never passed any stands of these on the way in. It was all softwoods."

Horsten realized that he was right. "Well we'll just find a turnaround cut, that's all." He spat again. "Keep your eyes peeled."

"Why did you say keep your eyes peeled?"

"Huh?"

"Well if you think the camp rumors are all, uh, bull . . ."

Horsten twisted to face him. "I meant for the right way back! What're you, numb? An' you didn't do that neither 'cause now we're on the wrong track."

The cab jolted, bringing the truck to an abrupt halt and throwing both men forward onto the dashboard.

"Goddammit!" Horsten yelled as he punched his fat, heavy hands into the steering wheel and pushed himself upright.

He opened the cab door and lowered himself to the road where ten inches of angular cut stump rose out of the dirt and into the wheel. Worse than a flat, the impact had punched a triangular indentation in the metal of the rim.

Horsten bit the web of skin between his thumb and forefinger in rage. The logging roads were supposed to be cut down to the dirt.

"Is everything okay?" McCloskey peeped from the cab.

"No, it ain't!" Horsten roared back.

He heard the passenger door open as McCloskey rounded the nose of the truck, a purple bruise already beginning to appear on his forehead.

"Oh damn," he said. "What's that smell?"

Horsten took two steps back towards the shoulder of the cut. Behind him, a steep slope of gravel and scrub extended for a hundred or so yards before ending at the tree line below. He heard the spatter of liquid hitting dirt and turning it to mud.

"Gas."

A creaking noise emanated from behind the cab. The collision had jaunted the trailer so that it pitched towards the men. The multi-ton weight of the load was now displaced against the few vertical metal ribs that held the stacked timber in place.

Horsten took another two steps back.

The straining rib furthest from the cab broke with a sharp pop. Sparks danced into life when the steel struck the metal edging of the trailer. The load shifted and the trailer swayed.

"Should I—" McCloskey's inquiry was cut short by the pop of another rib giving way. An errant spark landed near Horsten's foot. The trailer tires on the opposite side of the road lifted off the ground.

Horsten lunged forward, grabbed McCloskey by the neck of his overcoat, and pulled him to the shoulder of the road. The smell of gasoline, ordinarily vaguely sweet to him, had turned offensive and cloying. He turned with McCloskey under his arm and without hesitation pushed him towards the slope and vaulted himself over the edge.

"RUN!"

His footing remained sure on the loose gravel until the third pop. A muffled *whumpf* was followed by a *ka-BOOM* that he felt before he heard. The hot, heavy hand of some invisible deity lifted him from behind before throwing him back to the earth with a force that sent him tumbling. He came to a bruised and battered, but blessedly not broken, stop near the foot of the slope. He raised his head in a stupefied daze.

Several logs, some partially aflame, barreled towards him from the overturned truck above. Despite the pain and shock, Horsten shot to his feet and turned to run the final distance to the tree line. A speedy, limping gait was the best he could manage. He fervently pitched towards an opening between two great oaks. His labored breathing sucked hot air as he pictured himself lying dead mere steps from the forest.

The visual forced him into overdrive, and he stopped only after he heard the shuddering *thock* of wood on wood near his heels. He turned and watched log after log slam into the forest edge. A haze of white smoke drifted towards him as dead leaves and underbrush caught fire.

"McCloskey!" he bellowed through cupped hands.

There was no response, and he was nowhere to be seen. Turning from the thickening smoke, Horsten coughed and stumbled his way deeper into the woods, back in the general direction of the logging camp and away from the fledgling blaze.

He had been going for over a mile when he came upon

the stream. He drank deeply from it and washed his face, rivulets of water running down his coarse beard. It was another six or so miles to camp, but he knew that he was downhill from the lake adjacent to it; following the stream would lead him there. Even at his pace, he would reach the others by nightfall.

Horsten sat on a fallen tree and checked his pockets. The money was still there, and so was his knife and tobacco. He was seating the chew in his gums and wondering if he would lose his job when he heard a splash upstream.

"McCloskey," he said, and then louder, "McCloskey!"

He stood up and limped along the winding bank. The yellow and green growth of spring thickened as he progressed upstream. Twice he had to backtrack and leave the stream's edge to get around a thicket of thorny rose bushes and a tangled knot of rhododendron. He called McCloskey's name several times but heard nothing in response.

He came to a pool in the center of a clearing after pushing his way through a thick patch of greenery. Briars clung to his clothing and beard and he was dusted in a lime green pollen. Horsten chided himself for expending so much effort in looking for McCloskey. It was he who had nearly gotten them killed to begin with.

Probably woulda been better now that I ain't gonna have a job, he thought. He sat on the bank and spat into the pool where a school of small fish roiled. Rolling his knuckles in the dirt and sparse grass he leaned an aching shoulder against a tree, one of a few that stood in the clearing.

"Black walnuts," he muttered, noting the spot. He knew that they produced a chemical that killed other plants; he also knew that black walnut fetched a fine price at the mills in Bangor.

Looking into the clear water he saw the brownish-red strains of his tobacco-laden saliva unfurl and dilute, becoming a translucent gyre of swirls and whorls interrupted by darting fish seeking a morsel.

He spat into the school again, but unlike his last offering the fish showed no interest. From above him a drop hit the water. Horsten watched the fish swarm the concentrated crimson as it diffused from its deep hue to red, and then from red to an ethereal pink before vanishing. He squinted at the pool in confusion.

Another drop hit the water, and the fish teemed with vigor. Horsten looked up and gasped, nearly swallowing his tobacco.

There was McCloskey, high on the trunk of the budding black walnut, arms outstretched on two horizontal branches. His head lay forward on his chest, overcoat stickily wet and glistening, and blood beaded on his lower lip. His barefoot legs were bent beneath him. Thin, whip-like creepers colored a rusted red bound his hands and feet, and a thick vine strapped his waist to the trunk. He had been crucified.

McCloskey slowly lifted his head and met Horsten's gaze through a mat of hair. He opened his mouth to speak, but all that came out was a gurgle of blood. It pattered on the water below like a light rain.

Horsten ran. He crashed through the forest like an enormous, blind bear, stumbling and bouncing off trees, driven past the limits of his physical aches by a deep primal fear for his own life.

Crypt Gnats

As he ran he saw flits and blurs through the green and brown on either side of him. A flash of mahogany skin and black hair here. A burst of white feathers or yellow war paint there. From behind him he could hear the swift, soft pad of feet.

There were too many, and he was too weary. He could not outrun them. He saw a break in the wood line to his left, and figuring that they would think he would seek cover deeper in the woods, he veered for it.

Horsten burst through the trees and spun to face the forest edge, drawing his knife. The bare rock beneath his feet gave way to the edge of a cliff close behind him. He was panting and slightly crouched in a familiar position to do battle.

"Come on then!" he roared. "Let's see you fight out in the open like men!"

His knife, defiance, and anger were the only weapons he had against crippling fear.

His eyes flitted along the tree line. Despite the bright light of the day, the woods were ominous and shadowed. He could see no movement, but he did hear it: a smooth, slithering sound over the dead leaves.

It grew louder, and Horsten was astonished to see red roots emerge from the forest edge. Several dozens of them, moving slow and fat like pythons in the cold. They probed the rock surface he stood on, seemingly unaware of his presence. He stood frozen, defiance and fear forgotten in the face of utter incomprehension.

The roots stopped a few feet short of him, still scraping and probing the rock. Then, they retreated to the trees, and one by one burrowed back into the earth.

Crypt Gnats

Horsten took a cautious step forward that was punctuated by a sharp crack. A jagged split in the rock appeared to his left, billowing dust up several inches off the ground. Within seconds, a similar fissure opened across the surface on his right. He lunged forward, realizing what was happening, but his body was batted back by a swinging root the width of his thigh that shot up from one of the cracks, knocking the wind out of him. He was on his back looking up at the cloudless blue sky and gasping for breath when a third crack appeared alongside his head.

With a rumble, the sky above him shifted as the rock sheared from the cliff face.

He came to with a painful hollowness of returning breath. The sky surrounded him, and he thought that he was still falling. Then he saw the roots that were wrapped around his midsection and felt them pulling upwards as the trees below drew further away.

Horsten was hoisted higher than the plateau of the cliff and bound to a post of dead timber that had been dragged from its grave in the forest and supplanted onto the rock. It stood out boldly, jutting forward over the edge like the bowsprit of a ship with him as its figurehead. The roots raised a crossbeam and his arms were lashed to it.

In the near distance, no more than a mile, Horsten saw a brown splotch breaking the green near an opal of deep blue. The logging camp by the lake, a stain upon the landscape. In the far distance he could see the smoke and industry of Bangor.

Below him, the roots that held tight to the base of the dead tree were overlaid by those rushing down along the face of the cliff in a teeming cascade. There seemed to be thousands of them. A few wormed into a barrow hole that had been exposed where the rock had split and emerged with hundreds of yellowed bones as old as the forest itself. The rest slithered to the ground below and disappeared through the trees, heading in the direction of the logging camp.

Horsten's shouts were cut off by a pair of ethereal hands that shot forth from behind his head. One clenched the sides of his jaw and held it open while the other withdrew the bills from his breast pocket and stuffed them into his mouth. His breathing grew labored. He once more heard footsteps, approaching from behind him. With a sharp, dry report his legs were broken. He slumped forward and began to asphyxiate.

The hands cradled his head and lifted it upwards. Since he had no breath to scream, all Horsten could do was realize how vast and unending the sky truly was.

———

Andrew Punzo lives near Newark, New Jersey where he attends law school. He wrote for Fordham University's the paper and graduated summa cum laude with degrees in history and sociology. Andrew is an avid outdoorsman and enjoys reading a wide variety of fiction. He has been published in Theme of Absence and Mindscapes Unimagined.

*Sometimes the ties that bind appear in
mysterious ways.*

Sisters

Jim Knipp

Lena shrieked when Bithaih first came to her.

She had never thought of herself as someone who shrieked. Nothing in her prior forty years of existence— not the charnel house in that village outside Tijuana, not the war-torn slums of Afghanistan where she photographed empty-eyed, limbless children by the dozen, not even that fire-swept mountaintop in Colorado, the bodies burned beyond recognition, fused to the very rock beneath them—had indicated that she was even capable of shrieking.

She had stumbled into this place, slid through the crack in the hillside to escape the baleful eye of the Saharan sun, and collapsed in the grainy twilight just inside the entrance. Even in her exhaustion, she noticed the faint images carved into the walls, and thought of photographs and lighting and ways she could document this forgotten place she had discovered. It was not a cave as she had originally thought, but a tomb. She glanced back at the sunlight streaming from the outside and shuddered.

Photographs could wait. If help didn't find her, this tomb would become hers.

And then the darkness had gathered around her. The very air in the tomb grew viscous and black and roiled like water in a teapot. Lena shrieked until she tasted blood in the back of her throat. If her knees hadn't given out, if she hadn't collapsed to the sand in abject horror, she would have run, screaming, from this place, back out into the desert. The shifting darkness coalesced, took the shape of some dollar store horror, all jutting teeth and broken bone partially obscured by fossilized linen. Sunlight from the entrance glinted from resin black as obsidian. The thing smelled like cinnamon and rot.

Lena tried to crawl away, holding her camera in front of her like a cross. Her trembling finger accidentally depressed the shutter button and filled the tomb with white light. For a brief moment, she saw the chamber as it might have been. Limestone glowed bright with painted figures. Torchlight glinted on a thousand golden surfaces. And a forgotten queen sat upon a throne.

The darkness returned, leaving only this thing crawling in the sand towards her. Before Lena could scream again, a soft voice filled the darkness between them.

"Please, sister, don't be afraid. I will not hurt you."

The words wove through the latticework of panic that had held her and drew her teetering back towards sanity. This was not the voice of a monster. It was kind, the voice of a tired woman who had borne an unimaginable burden for far too long. The air in the tomb grew colder, and Lena felt something pulled from her, like smoke drifting through a chimney. Her vision flickered, and again the image of a queen sat before her. Straight black hair streamed to her shoulders. Her black eyes glowed fierce and regal. Beneath this image lay a core of shadow, broken and dark, a reminder of what had crawled through the sand moments before.

The queen spoke again, her voice heavy with regret.

"I am sorry to take from you sister."

"I . . . I don't understand." Lena whispered. Her throat felt shredded, like she had swallowed glass.

"My true appearance is not conducive to conversation," Bithaih continued. "I've drawn a sort of energy from you to supplement my own . . . to make it easier to talk."

The queen motioned, an invitation to draw closer. Lena hesitated for moment, and then crawled through the cold sand and sat with her back pressed against the gritty sandstone walls of the tomb.

"I am Bithaih, and I ruled these lands when they were green and the gods still walked among men."

Images filled Lena's mind, an oasis that stretched for miles, a beloved queen who walked amongst her people like a living goddess, and a cadre of angry men who preached resentful sermons about a woman's rightful place.

"They had angered me," Bithaih murmured. "So I sent them into the desert, branded them as traitors. I did not know that they had planted a seed. I did not know that they had turned my own brother against me."

The images grew darker. Men led Bithaih away in chains; a scarred priest chanted indescribable words that sent waves of nausea crashing into Lena from across the eons, a queen screamed in anger and frustration as her very essence turned to black ichor and blended into the darkness.

"I cursed them as I died, and I called upon the gods to avenge me. They did. The betrayers were betrayed. Armies came, and with them came slaughter and sand. It covered everything and left me in this tomb to walk in darkness forever, forgotten."

Bithaih sighed. A black tear crawled down her porcelain cheek and evaporated into the darkness.

Lena imagined walking this tomb alone for a dozen millennia. The sheer weight of that time pressed upon her, and she took the queen's hand.

Cold poured into her, and with it, that connection, that sense of draining. Memories and images flooded through her.

Lena in the newsroom, finally declining another assignment, Carpenter's mocking smirk as he assumed she had finally broke. She remembered their first meeting, when he lectured her about the fitness of women journalists.

"Stay in your lane and let the men work," he had muttered. How she wanted to punch that smug face. Instead she had taken every assignment, no matter where it took her, no matter what it cost.

Unbidden, she thought of those places: Afghanistan, Mexico, Iraq. She had always kept those memories buried deep within her, an internal crypt where they could fester in darkness, brought forth only when sleep was scarce and she was unable to drown them in a bottle. Now they were drawn from her, images of bodies piled like cordwood, souls torn asunder.

"Is that all this world is?" Bithaih wept. "So much darkness?"

But as dark as the world was, there was also wonder and light. Lena focused and thought of the many things that had brought her joy.

Her first look of New York, that vibrant city of light unfolded before her with infinite possibility. Her first foreign assignment. The view from the Sun Gate at Machu Picchu, mountains unfurling around the walls of that ancient city like something from a children's storybook. The view of the Mediterranean from 30,000 feet, the gleaming blue waters and white shores teeming with secrets. Mauna Loa raining fire and filling the sky with impossible colors. The slow muddy waters of the Amazon and the smiling children who lovingly wove white feathers into her hair. The wonders of the market in Cairo, the crush of humanity, the myriad of colors, a miasma of a thousand scents— spices, sweat, diesel, the pungent smell of acacia flowers blooming outside her hotel.

"Sister, you must stop."

More memories poured out. She and Taylor as children, Lena snapping photo after photo of her younger sister as they giggled and shared secret dreams. Lena's to photograph the world, Taylor's to delve into history, to search secret tombs and solve mysteries lost in time. She remembered the posters above Taylor's bed, the pyramids at Giza, the Sphinx, Tutankhamen's mask. Places she never got a chance to see . . .

Lena, please, let me go.

Bithaih's voice, echoed by Taylor's. Taylor, from the hospital bed. Taylor transformed during Lena's long journeys into a wraith buried beneath tubes and sensors. How many years had she held off seeing her sister while chasing just one more assignment? How many opportunities had she missed to share during her sister's short life, all to shut up Carpenter's smug voice?

"It's okay," Taylor had whispered, as Lena cried at her bedside. "We followed our own paths. Lena, let me go."

Lena released Bithaih's hand and flung herself away from the queen. The world spun and Lena dropped to her knees. Her heart hammered against her rib cage like a frightened bird, her breath came in spastic spurts.

Bithaih stood, nearly solid, the shadow of her broken form completely obscured. Her eyes flashed with naked hunger, and she moved closer to Lena, arm outstretched. Lena reached out, wanting to make that connection again, willing to give everything to bring her sister back. Concern crossed Bithaih's face and she stepped away.

"No," she said. "If I take more, you will die. Leave. Now."

Lena struggled to her feet, the world before her covered in gauze. She stumbled forward. The sliver of light that marked the entrance seemed a mile away. She turned. Bithaih had already begun to fade into shadow.

"Go, sister. Follow your own path."

Lena slipped through the crack in the entrance and fell into blinding sunlight. She lay there until the hot sand burned the skin of her face and the palms of her hands. She dragged herself up to a nearby rock. The sunlight drove away the tomb's chill. Her strength slowly returned. She turned. The entranceway to Bithaih's tomb had disappeared, obscured by sun and sand. Voices called her name from over the hillside. Her tour group had found her. She was no longer lost.

She didn't know whether Bithaih truly wandered the darkness below the sand, or if she was just a dream, brought forth by dehydration and regret. Perhaps it didn't matter, because Lena had found her place and her purpose: To reflect on the world, to remember her sister, to share in her light and help—if only for a moment—lift another out of darkness.

Jim Knipp is the author of "Stuff Every Grandfather Should Know" (Quirk) He has published stories in the anthologies "Tall Tales and Short Stories from South Jersey" and "In a Flash." His flash piece "Mr. Belial" was published in Philly Flash Inferno. Jim is a member of the South Jersey Writers' group and serves on the Board of Directors of the Philadelphia Writers' Conference. He sometimes remembers to update his blog at www.knippknopp.com and provides recaps for Game of Thrones and other pop commentary over at Biff Bam Pop. Jim lives in the wilds of Southern New Jersey with a very patient wife who has put up with more 2 AM 'what If scenarios and story ideas then any person ever deserves.

The sense of smell can reveal many hidden secrets in this tale.

Smell of Stone

Agnieszka Kwiatkowska
Translated by Magdalena Malek

"You are such a freak," said Monica, and that was the beginning of an end. Fewer and fewer honest smiles, less and less time for me, more and more meetings with friends. So when she started a conversation with "I've thought about us a lot and I'm not sure if there's any point in this," I interrupted her and said that she was right, there was no point; I broke up with her, getting ahead of her move.

A couple of days later I returned home to the village in the outskirts of Rovigo in Italy, to my father. I'd finished the fourth year of my studies in Padua and I was free.

The first night home, I went for a hike. I'd thought the exhausting day and the journey would affect me and that I would sleep through the entire night in my own bed.

When I sat down to eat supper with my father, my head hurt and I could hardly keep my eyes open. It was dark and cool in the kitchen, and the conversation was heavy going. My father seemed to blend in with the semi-darkness. The lights went off again, so we lit the kitchen with candles. It was then, despite the exhaustion, that I felt that gentle call all over in my body, the call that I responded to so many times.

I ignored it and went to bed, still dressed. I felt my unease grow. I stood up, paced around the room, went for a cup of hot tea to the kitchen. In the end I left the house, and as soon as I was out, I followed the lead of my legs that seemed to have a mind of their own, and I walked towards the cemetery. The night was quiet and warm; I was there after fifteen minutes of a slow walk. I looked around as usual and climbed up the low wall with ease. I jumped down to the ground and straightened up. I was in the corner of the cemetery, just next to the Fabresi family crypt.

Suddenly, everything went dark; the clouds crossing the sky obscured the moon. I closed my eyes; I stretched my arm forward. I could feel the shape of the stone sculpture decorating the crypt under my fingers. I put my cheek against the angel's cool wing. I breathed in the smell of stone with delight.

Ever since I was a small child, I knew that I was different. My mother thought I was fooling around when I was picking up rocks and stones and smelling them whenever we went out for a walk. I explained that they smell beautifully, but she only shook her head and laughed. She told me that stones have no smell, but I thought she was teasing me, because for me, stones were full of smells, sensations, and memories. Cars and carts had been driven over those stones; people had walked over them. I didn't see them in the stones, but I could feel them.

Crypt Gnats

On my way to school, I used to intentionally take the longer route, so that I could pass by the cemetery. My sense of smell was quite well-developed at that time and all I needed was to walk slowly, breathing in the smell of the wall. It was an effort to stop myself from going through that gate, walking along the alleys and enjoying the smell of the stone slabs of the graves.

I realized that I need to be careful when I was twelve. My parents and I took a trip to Padua to visit the grave of my grandparents. I lit a candle and bowed my head to pray and then I felt dizzy. The stone slab smelled first of coldness and dampness, but then the smell changed to the smell of the sun, grandma's warm skin, her soap, grandpa's tobacco, his rough beard, deeper, and deeper . . . .

My father picked me up with a sharp pull when I lay down on the slab and put my cheek on it. He struggled to take me out of the cemetery as I tried to break free; I didn't want to leave.

"I didn't know that you would take it so hard," said my mother in the evening as she was bustling about the kitchen. I sat there silently, trying to understand what had just happened. I picked on the piece of cake that I had never before been allowed to eat for supper.

My father was not angry; he simply said nothing. He ate the supper in silence.

What a relief it was when I was finally told to go to my room! I went up the stairs, and as soon as I was certain that nobody could see me at the mezzanine, I leaned so that my nose would be close to the rail and I started to smell it. It smelled of wood. Just wood. There were no layers underneath, no depth, nothing. Metal, paper, cloth-

ing—they smelled the same. Like metal, paper, and clothing.

But when I left the house the next day and I smelled
the stone foundation . . . the stone smelled like mother's
tenderness, father's taciturnity, a young wife's joy and unease, dog hair, and jazz music.

I knew that I could go deeper into this extravaganza
of experiences and memories. But I didn't want to, even
though I was tempted. I didn't want to interfere with my
parents' life and feelings. That would be . . . gross. But
stones along the road? Statues? Graves? They hid memories of people that I didn't know.

***

I left the cemetery the same way that I got in, over
the wall, when it was still dark. Nobody had noticed me
for so many years; I was careful. The cemetery was quite
out of the way, and the asphalt road leading to it was on
the other side. Here I had a well-trodden path which led
to the fields on one side and to the forest on the other
side. There were hardly any people walking it, at night
in particular.

I jumped over the wall; I shook off my hands; I zipped
up my sweater so that my neck was covered. It was cold.
The clouds raced along the sky, obscuring or revealing the
moon as they pleased. I started going back, sometimes not
even seeing the path and walking blindly.

It was so dark in the small forest that I nearly fell
down a couple of times. When I reached home—a large,
rectangular building—I noticed that the lights were on in
my father's room. I grimaced and hesitated. I wasn't too
keen on trying to explain to my father why I wandered off

outside at three in the morning, but all in all, I has been an adult for a long time already. But I hesitated anyway. I walked up to the wall and knelt down, my parents blending with the stone foundation.

Years ago, I had promised myself that I would never ever read my parents' memories. But my mother had been dead for two years. And as a sign of respect, I had never touched her gravestone slab. I wanted her memory to remain pristine in my mind.

But I always carried sorrow and sadness. My father told me she died calmly and quietly, in her bed a couple of days after I went back to the university. And I was plagued by the fact that I had never said a proper goodbye. It was like, "Bye Mum. I'll come by one weekend." And I knew she had a heart condition.

I placed my hands on the foundation and put my forehead on the cool stones. And I began to absorb the house.

For the first time ever I consciously searched for a specific person in the smell of stone. Up until that point, I absorbed feelings without any filtering; now I focused on my mother. After a longer while, she began to be visible in the kaleidoscope of emotions and sensations. The lavender soap shyly emerged from underneath my father's cigarettes and his leather shoes. The creaking floor under her steps, mornings when her hands woke me up to go to school. I absorbed my mother, her feelings, her emotions, the very essence of her being, with all my might.

It was only then that I understood how often she had a migraine, though she never complained. I had remembered her as a healthy, energetic, and powerful person, but now I could feel her suffering—the headache that almost split the skull in two, nausea, heavy and swollen legs, bleeding, and despair.

Mother lost a child! Emotions and sensations swirled in my head; I wasn't able to stop them. I absorbed the house, but the house absorbed me, too. We merged into one, I wanted to reject it, push it away, but I couldn't. The house became Mother, Mother became me.

Emotions and sensations flooded me like a wave. I wasn't able to control them; they poured right through me, without any order. Laughter and tears, joy and sadness, child's first steps, sunrise over Po, and a long corridor with wavy walls, twisting and turning like a snake, distorted by the sickness gnawing on the walls. The weak heart that crumbled down mother's health from the inside, taking her breath away, painting her hair silver. Deeper and deeper wrinkles, scraped and scratched by worries.

Something alien disturbed the lavender smell of my mother. The lavender faded away, giving way to the smell of soil that filled my senses. I felt her struggle, the fight to breathe, but then it all slowly dissipated into the bedding that was warm from being slept in. Then stillness.

And I woke up with a start. The stream of emotions ended; I was lying on my back, with my head against a stone sticking out from the ground. For a while I felt as if I went deaf, so striking was the difference between the cool June night and the things that I had absorbed from the house. Slowly, everything went back to as it had been before: the moon was peeking from behind the clouds, the wind was blowing in the crowns of the trees, and I was lying on the ground in front of my house, in the real world.

My father was walking up to me. I sat up with dif-

Crypt Gnats

ficulty, brutally brought back to reality, carrying the full awareness how much that reality changed. I saw the silhouette of my father from the backdrop of the light that was on at the main entrance. With each of his steps, new sensations reached my brain.

"What are you doing?" My father leaned over me, and I knew everything right there and then. I felt the smell of his cigarettes, the wine that he had drank at noon, his shaving cream. And I went deeper. For the first time, ever, I could feel a human being just as they are, inside. I closed my eyes. He smelled of unease and irritation, and deeper, deeper still, he carried that well-preserved fear in him, so that nobody would know how tired and discouraged he was. The bitterness of arguments, the consuming aversion, the sense of being trapped in a cage . . . .

That soft waft of a woman's body, of youth and perfume, hid somewhere deep there—delicate, but strong enough that it was impossible to get rid of. And deeper, deeper still . . . .

Now, for the first time ever, I absorbed a living human being.

"Son, get up. I will take you inside," said that thing that used to be my father, and now became just a smell. The smell of death and hands holding the pillow which had swallowed the last breath of my mother. Forever.

———◆———

Agnieszka Kwiatkowska (born in 1978 in Warsaw, Poland). She's an author of several horror and ghost stories. She published on magazines like Histeria, OkoLica Strachu,and in a few anthologies. In 2017 she published her first book, Drugi Peron, which included 7 stories and got nominated for Stefan Grabinski's Award (Polish award for horror fiction). When she doesn't write, she works as a manicurist, cooks and takes care of her pets (snails and fish). Loves coffee, Italy and good books. That's the first publication in the U.S. She was also published in Czech Republic in Howard Magazine. This story was translated by Magdalena Malek.

Death sometimes bring families
closer together.

Just Like Daddy

Hillary Lyon

"Why are you still digging in the garden, Wendell?"
Ma stood on the back porch and crossed her arms, something she always did when she was insecure. The longer
she waited for an answer, the lower the corners of her
mouth drooped.

Wendell looked over the edge of the hole and wiped
his sweaty forehead with the back of his hand, leaving a
smear across his face like earthy warpaint. "Ma, I got to
dig a proper grave for Daddy. You know that." He put his
head down and recommenced digging.

Ma sighed. Her boy was so stubborn; just like his daddy. When he made up his mind about something, that was
that. He made a plan and carried it through.

"Land sakes alive! You know the county's not going to
let you bury him in our backyard. You're just gonna make
trouble for all of us."

Her son pulled himself up and sat on the edge of
the gaping hole, dangling his legs. He put his hands behind him and leaned back, squinting up at the sunshine

through the trees. He liked the way it shifted through the leaves with every little breeze, making patterns of alternating bright green, black shade, and glints of blinding light. "The county won't know if you don't tell them." He lay back on the cool grass, his legs still hanging over the hole's edge. "They don't need to know all our business. Besides, I thought this would make you happy."

Ma threw up her hands. "It does, son, but just how deep are you planning to go? To China? Looks like you could stop digging any time now. And it's so wide—like a swimming pool! That's a huge hole! Your daddy wasn't a big man—especially not at the end."

Wendell sat up and looked down at the gaping hole before him. He suppressed a laugh; his septuagenarian mother was always so dramatic. It was her default setting, he supposed. "I know. But we don't want any critters sniffing around here, digging 'em up." He turned and looked at his mother. "Do we?"

Ma snorted and folded her arms again. "Your big sister will be home for dinner tonight—home for the first time in thirty-five years. Flying in all the way from London. Remember, you promised me you'd try to talk some sense into her about staying here and helping take care of me. I will not go into an old folks' home—they reek of urine and death! Linoleum-lined Hells." She raised her chin in defiance. "I spent what was left of my youth taking care of you two—and I didn't mind, you were my babies after all—but the whole time your daddy played the field like he was a bachelor—"

"Ma," Wendell interrupted. "I know all this—"

"And your big sister acts just like him! No body matters but Sissy! It's long past time she learns different." Ma balled her fists and stuck them on her hips. "If she turns a deaf ear to you, you do what needs to be done. Handle her just like you handled your daddy when he stopped listening to us." She turned and walked back to the old house. The screen door slammed behind her. "Make sure your hands are washed and your nails are clean before you come to the supper table. Be presentable for your sister."

Dinner together, just like old times. Except Daddy was in the ground. Sissy didn't know that; well, she knew her father had passed, but she assumed he'd been interred in the old family plot in the cemetery on the edge of town. She was overseas when her Daddy died and had pulled all manner of strings to get home as soon as she could, which was a full week after the event. Wendell understood; sometimes situations made you an indentured servant. Ma, on the other hand, didn't understand, and saw no benefit in trying.

As Ma always did on special occasions—and Sissy being back from London was a special occasion for Ma—she cooked more food than was needed, or wanted, so Wendell and Sissy both ate too much. But their mother would have been disappointed if they'd refused a second or third helping. And they couldn't disappoint their mother, not at a time like this.

They didn't say much during the meal; Wendell decided he'd converse with his sister after their mother went to bed. So silverware clanked against plates, and someone occasionally cleared their throat, or softly said between mouthfuls, "Mmmm, this certainly is good, Ma."

After his last bite of cherry pie, Wendell said, "Don't

worry about clean up, Ma. Me and Sissy will take care of it."

Sissy pushed her chair away from the table. "You go on upstairs and try to get some sleep, Ma. I've got jet lag, and the time change is playing havoc with my body clock. So I'll be wide awake for a while." She tilted her head and smiled at her mother—a mannerism Sissy had adopted as child because her parents, Daddy in particular, had found it so endearing. When little Wendell did the same, his father told him to sit up straight, and then asked him if he had an earache.

The old woman primly wiped the corners of her mouth. "I suppose I will. But Sissy dear, it's been so long since I've seen you." She glanced over at Wendell. "But I know you two have lots to talk about, things your gray old momma would be mortified to hear!" She laughed conspiratorially.

"It's alright, Ma. I'm going to be here for a while, so don't fret. Go on to bed; it's okay." Sissy reached out and patted her mother's wrinkled hand. Wendell noticed Sissy wasn't wearing her engagement ring. Looks like his sister had dumped another beau. This would be, what? The third or fourth broken engagement? No boyfriend ever fully met her standard, which was based on her daddy. In the long run, like her father, they always let her down her, in one way or another.

"Well, I am awfully tired, honey." The old woman sighed happily. "It's just wonderful to have you home again! It's like a good dream after a nightmare." She dabbed a with Gather somehow

the corner of her eye. As she walked out of the dining

room, she glanced back over her shoulder and said, "Son, thank you for taking care of your sister—and everything. I hope you know how much I do appreciate it."

When they heard her step on the topmost stair, which creaked loudest, Wendell turned to his sister and whispered, "Come outside with me, so we can talk. And there's something I want to show you."

Once in the backyard, Wendell led his sister through the burgeoning twilight to what had once been their mother's small vegetable garden, but was now a large, deep hole, partially filled in. He picked up his shovel and leaned on it.

"I noticed there's no ring on your finger. What happened with Toby?" Not that he really cared hearing about yet another one of her romantic dramas, which was almost all she talked about when she called them thrice a year. He felt it was his duty as her brother to ask. Fifty-four years old and Sissy was still unable to commit to another person. He spit into the dark pit before them.

Sissy ran her hands through her short dyed-blonde hair. A nervous habit. "Toby said he felt powerless in our relationship," she laughed bitterly. "I know, I know. Everyone said there'd be trouble if I fell for a man fifteen years younger, but he was so..." she sighed. "Anyway, in order to regain said power, he took to sleeping around with every pert little intern than crossed his path, because sticking his—"

"When you moved away to London, it broke Ma's heart," Wendell interrupted. "Daddy's too, though he kept it hidden. Of course, they were proud of you, as Daddy told anybody who'd listen, and some who wouldn't." He shifted his weight on the shovel. "His college girl, making a big career for herself overseas. The bright star on the top of their Christmas tree."

Sissy turned and looked at Wendell's shadowed face. "It's getting dark out here, and chilly. I want to go inside. What do you want to show me?"

He ignored her. "I was accepted at Wrangler State. Was gonna study business administration. Had a slot in the dorm and everything. Then Daddy had his first heart attack. So I got to stay here instead and help out in the family business. Been stuck here for over thirty years! When I had to drop out of college, George Bush the First was president! Christ, it feels like a whole lifetime ago. And remember cute little Cindy Miller, my high school sweetheart? The love of my life? She went away to Wrangler and met some smooth frat boy, and that's all she wrote. Did you know all that?"

"No, I don't think so, I—" Obviously uncomfortable now with the direction of their conversation, he watched as she turned away to stare at the curious hole, at the starlight emerging through the gaps in the leaves overhead, at the neighbor's back porch light that just snapped on.

"No, you were too wrapped up in Sissy," Wendell said, still gripping the shovel, and slyly stepped behind her. "Ma and I have decided you need to stop being so self-centered—you need to stay here now for Mom."

Sissy shuddered. "You said Daddy's first heart attack. How many did he suffer? Is that what killed him?"

"No," Wendell said as he raised the shovel like a baseball bat, "this is."

***

Early the next morning, as Ma prepared a gargantuan breakfast, she looked out the kitchen window and saw Wendell walking back up to the house from the garden. She could see the hole was filled in. She sighed with relief. But now, what had been her little veggie garden was such an ugly dark spot in her otherwise manicured backyard! Maybe Wendell would plant some azalea bushes there for her. After all, she supposed now the soil would be well fertilized. And a burst of pink or purple flowers would likely cheer up that depressing spot, wouldn't it?

"Be sure to wipe your feet before you waltz into my spotless kitchen!" Ma called out as Wendell opened the backdoor. "I know you worked up an appetite, what with filling in that hole so quickly—and thank you for that!" She beamed at Wendell. "Such a good boy! Always working so hard to please your old mother."

She hugged him before turning back to the stove. "Will Sissy be joining us for breakfast? Did you talk some sense into her last night? Or did you have to—is she—"

"Nah," Wendell answered, washing his hands in the kitchen sink before picking up a piece of extra crispy bacon. "For all her brains, and she obviously had a lot, she wasn't a very good listener." Wendell laughed.

Taking a hot pan of her cheese biscuits out of the oven, Ma asked, "So does this mean Sissy will finally stay put, here at home?" Ma placed a big bowl of steaming scrambled eggs on the table before him and handed him a serving spoon.

"Most definitely, Ma," Wendell said as he scooped a generous helping of eggs onto his plate. "She's not going anywhere."

Ma wiped a tear from her eye and said, "Just like your daddy?"

Wendell stopped eating, handed her a tissue and said, "Exactly."

———◆———

Having earned an MA in English Literature from SMU ages ago, Hillary Lyon founded in 2000 and continues to serve as senior editor for the independent poetry publisher, Subsynchronous Press. She began writing fiction in earnest 10 years ago, and her stories now have appeared in nearly 50 publications. She's also an illustrator for horror & pulp fiction magazines. She has had stories published in Night to Dawn, Tales from the Moon Lit Path and The Sirens Call
When not writing or illustrating, she hand-paints furniture in the colorful Dia del los Muertos style. Having lived in France, Brazil, Canada, and several states in the US, she currently resides in southern Arizona.

*A story that shows that probing into the past
can sometimes affect the present.*

Uncovering a Body

S. Gepp

The rocky promontory jutted out into the sea, a thin piece of land that was all that was left of a weather-beaten headland. The local geologists had given it no more than ten years before the last remnants of it crashed down into the sea, and so the five men standing on top, with shovels in their hands, knew they had very little time before this whole area would be too dangerous for them to work on.

Dr. Anthony McGrath looked across at the excavations they had completed so far. What little was left of the ancient Roman temple seemed to have all been uncovered and documented, but now they had to go lower and find out what, if anything, lay beneath. The Romans were notorious for building their places of worship on top of those of the local peoples, and he was hoping to find some evidence of this having happened here.

"So, what do we do first?" asked Badger, who was an undergraduate student from the University of Kent.

"I'm not sure," he replied. "We seem to only have the southern end of the temple complex remaining, so I'm not even sure there will be any more ancient remains under-neath it."

"Maybe we should dig down outside and find the foundations," Enos suggested. He was a middle-aged American who had been working the Roman ruins in the area for more than a decade.

"Why?" Badger asked, genuinely curious.

Enos smiled at him. "Even though there's no mosaics or anything, I still don't want to break into the floor inside the temple itself until we absolutely have to. Maybe we'll find evidence of a hypocaust, and then we can open up the floor and see one in situ. If we know what we're going to find under the floor, all the better. We'll know how careful we have to be."

The others all shrugged and nodded their agreement, and so, with small spades and trowels at the ready, they started to scrape away at the main wall they had discov-ered. They dug lower and lower for the entire morning un-til Anthony called a halt to proceedings.

Anthony pulled out a tape measure and looked at the depth they had gone, then repeated it on the inside of the temple. "That's strange," he muttered.

"What is it?" Badger asked.

"Well, we haven't found the foundations yet, or any air vents or anything. This is all still external wall," An-thony explained, "and yet out here we're already a metre lower than the floor level in there." He faced Enos. "Seen this before around here?" he asked.

"Not at all," was the curious response.

"I have," said Georges, one of the other archaeologists. "In Cornwall. It was a Roman temple, like this, but built not long before the Romans left. The raised floor got us talking as well, and then one of the grad students dropped his pickaxe on it." He smiled with a curious, little smirk. "It was hollow."

"What?" Anthony peered over the wall at the floor.

"What was in it?" Badger asked.

"Not a great deal. It was empty apart from a few pieces of jewelry. See, we also found a hole in the wall at one end that had been filled in," Georges said. "Thieves got to it first."

"But this time th' whole other end o' th' floor is missing, somewhere down in th' sea," Gareth, the final member of the quintet said. "So we don' know if anyone's been in't or not."

Georges said nothing, but instead walked to the far end of the uncovered ruins. He carefully dropped down and started to scrape away at the crumbling end. After a few minutes he returned to the rest. "There is nothing there but dirt. No hollow," he said.

"So?" Anthony was still eager.

"Well . . . ." He reached down and took the shovel from Badger's hand and brought it down as hard as he could against the floor at his feet. He brought it down again and again and then stepped back quickly as the sounds of something crashing reached the ears of everyone else. They climbed quickly over the wall and stared at the hole he had created. "It's here," he laughed.

Within half an hour the floor over what was quite a substantial hollow underneath floor had been removed, revealing a dark chasm. "What now?" Badger asked.

"Well, it's empty," Gareth sighed. "We were beaten to it."

Anthony did not respond, but instead carefully sat on the edge and dropped down. He landed and stood up, his head just above the level of the floor. "Have we got a torch somewhere?" he asked.

Badger jumped back to the equipment on the other side of the wall and returned a few moments later with an old flashlight. He handed it to Anthony who ducked down and disappeared beneath the floor. He reappeared quickly. "We need to keep moving the floor," he said.

"What is it?" Georges asked.

He grinned. "I think it's a sarcophagus."

***

By midafternoon the floor had been removed above the large, empty section of the temple, revealing a solitary stone sarcophagus. With small brushes they carefully cleaned the buildup of two thousand years of dirt and dust from the marble surface. Letters appeared across the lid, and the carving of a head and upper body was revealed at one end.

Enos stopped sweeping and used a squeeze bottle to wash the final dirt from the face and then stepped back. "Hey, come here," he said to Badger.

The younger man came across and gasped. Gareth was soon with them and it was his laughter that brought the other two over. "Hey!" Georges said. "That's you!"

All of them turned and stared at Anthony. He looked at each of them uncomfortably, then forced a smile onto his face. "Yeah, sure," he said. "Maybe some peripheral similarities, but you guys just see what you want to see. You know, something we're warned about all the time when we're searching in the field."

Smiles were not returned. Instead Badger and Enos cleaned the face a little more. "This is really eerie," Enos muttered. "I mean, seriously, Anthony—this guy is the spitting image of you."

"Coincidence. Confirmation bias," Anthony growled. "I'll admit there is some similarity, but you now have it in your minds. We are scientists, not incredulous morons. What next? The face of Jesus in your paella?"

They bowed their heads a little and, without further words, returned to their work. But it was only Enos who recognized what he saw in the expedition's leader—he was shaken rather badly.

"Who's the Latin scholar?" Badger suddenly called.

Both Enos and Anthony approached him, but Enos held back to let the other man get there first, to take his mind off the image at the opposite end of the stone structure. "Where is it?' he asked.

"Across the lid. I think I've got all the words," Badger said.

Anthony ran his fingers beneath the well-formed lettering. "*Hic Antonius iacet*," he read. "Here lies Antonius . . ." His voice faded and he stumbled back.

"Here lies Antonius," Enos repeated, taking over. "He fell in the sea from the sky . . . ."

"It doesn't say that," Anthony whispered.

"*In mare de caelo ruit*," Enos read out. "What else could it be?"

Anthony shook his head.

"*Nautis eripuit*. He was rescued by sailors. *Ab loco dissimilis erat*. He was from a different place," Enos went on. "*Uixit per annos tres*. He lived for three years. *Rexit benigne*. He ruled kindly. *Haec domus eius est*. This is his home or temple." He stared at the words, then at the carved face. Everyone else was staring at him.

Enos had to do something to break the mood, so he burst out laughing. "Wow," he said, "this is some story. Guys, we've got some sort of ruler here, one with a very strange myth attached to him. We might need to hit the local libraries to find out what it actually means."

"He's important, too," Georges added. "I mean, they built a whole temple for him."

"I think we should look inside this," Anthony said suddenly, touching the stone casket.

"What?" Enos said. "I don't think that's a good . . ."

"This whole place will be gone in a few years. If we don't have a look at him, then he'll be gone forever, as well as whatever he might have in there with him." Anthony came back to the structure and squatted down to look at the edge. It was decorated with a vine motif but there was a definite crack where it had been cemented shut, a line just beneath the lid that had caused him so much angst. He looked at the sky and the low sun. "We'll come back tomorrow with the tools to open it up."

"Fair enough," Enos agreed, and they covered the structure with plastic sheeting before packing their gear and heading back along the narrow path before the darkness made it too dangerous.

***

Enos could not sleep. He tossed and turned in bed, and even having some boring infomercial on the television did not help.

It was that burial site. That face was so much like Anthony's, and then there was the name as well. It was such a huge coincidence, and that was all it was, but there was something about it that still felt wrong.

It wouldn't leave him. In more than twenty years of working in the field, this was only the second time he had ever been affected this badly by a site, and the last had been the children's mass grave from the plague era they had found near the town of Braintree. This was not even close to the horrors in that pit beneath the proposed site of a new playground, and yet he felt exactly the same.

He wandered across to the window of the hotel room and stared out over the sea towards the narrow promontory. His heart stuck in his throat. On this cloudy night, when even the glow from the moon barely illuminated the scene, the dot of light moving over there stood out like a beacon.

Someone was walking over there. He watched, not sure what he was waiting for, when it suddenly disappeared. Just like that.

A shudder ran through him.

What had he just seen? A tomb robber? He needed to go to Anthony's room, wake him up, and see what they could do.

***

The four men stood in the doorway of the empty room. "Where is he?" Badger asked nervously, breaking the silence.

Enos looked at the window on the far side of the room and the open curtains. "I know," he growled.

"So what does he think he's doing?" Georges asked with a shake of his head.

None of them had an answer. But they all knew what they were going to do next.

**

"Why are you doing this?"

Anthony turned with a start as the four men stepped into his line of sight. He dropped the large tyre lever in his hands and stepped back a few paces, his mouth opening and closing, but no words came out.

Enos looked at his companions, and then jumped down next to the older man. "Why are you doing this?" he repeated.

Anthony shrugged. "I had a dream," he finally muttered. "I saw this place when it was a wide piece of land, before there was a temple, before the weather wore it down to nothing." He looked at the cracks he had already made in the lid. "I don't know what I was thinking to come out here . . ."

"You want t' make sure it's not you in there, aye," Gareth muttered, also jumping down. He set his torch up on the edge of the hole they had made and picked up the tyre lever. "I don' think you're goin' t' do much wi' t'is."

Anthony shrugged.

Enos sighed and looked up at the other two. Badger pulled out a battery-powered circular saw and passed it down to Gareth. Within moments he was working at the line of concrete that marked where the lid had been sealed down.

Finally, all five of the men leant against the lid and after some resistance, with the grinding of stone on stone, it started to slide sideways. "That's enough!" Enos called. "We don't want to break it."

They stood around and stared at the opening, none daring to gaze inside. Finally, Badger edged his way forward and peered in. He groaned and shook his head with a slight smile. The rest all made their way forward and relaxed immediately. "I don't know what we were expecting," Enos said. "After two millennia, what else was going to be in here?"

The grinning skull and yellowed bones were clad in the remains of rags, but that was all they could see. It was just another well-preserved skeleton of some long-dead ruler. Badger lifted his torch and shone it down the length of the body. "What's this?" he muttered and reached down to the pelvis.

He handed the torch to Georges and reached in with both hands. He carefully pulled out something which was about the size of one palm. "What's that?" Enos asked.

"It's a metal tin, but it's rusted shut." He tried the lid. "It feels like it's breaking. We should take it back and try to open it, but I wouldn't to do it here without . . . ." His voice faded as Anthony climbed out of the hole and started to walk away from them all.

"What's wrong?" Georges called.

Anthony said nothing. He merely reached into his back pocket and pulled out a metal tin. It looked like a clean version of the one in Badger's hand.

"What is it?" Enos asked.

"I used this instead of a wallet," he whispered.

"Come on," Enos said, forcing a smile onto his face and approaching the team leader. "Another coincidence."

Anthony moved backwards away from him, eyes wide, shaking his head slowly.

"It is just a coincidence," Enos continued. "What else could it be?"

Anthony shook his head a little more firmly and took another pace backwards, shoving his tin back into his pocket.

The ground beneath him crumbled. He teetered there briefly, then started to flail his arms about before he tumbled backwards and disappeared from view completely. Enos rushed to the edge of the cliff as the rest clambered out of the hole in a mad panic to join him.

Anthony stared at them . . . and then he was gone.

"Where'd he go?" Georges asked urgently.

Enos just shook his head.

Not even the telltale sign of a splash could be seen on the surface of the water. He'd just disappeared into thin air.

Badger looked at the tin in his hand and cracked the seal around its edge. The rusted metal crumbled a little beneath the force of his touch, but he managed to keep hold of it all in his palm.

He shifted the top layer of crumbling and faded paper.

The laminated plastic was also faded, but the image from the photograph staring back at them was instantly recognizable. And the name on the identification card was one they all knew.

They peered down at the sea below.

Without saying another word, Badger threw Dr. Anthony McGrath's two-thousand-year-old personal effects after his body.

S. Gepp is an Australian, with two children, two university degrees (and counting), two tertiary education diplomas, and a resumé that looks like a list of every job you could ever have without really trying, including stints as a school teacher, scientist, editor and journalist. He has also been a performance acrobat, a professional wrestler, a stand-up comedian and an actor. He has been writing for 30 years with some publications: one novella, about 10 poems, 40-odd short stories, including Lovecraftiana magazine, Candlemas 2019, A To Z Cities of Death and Use Enough Gun: Tales Of The Monster Hunter III. He hopes to be a real writer if he grows up. A dull life.

Making love in a graveyard can prove to be a sticky situation.

The Blood of the Tree

John C. Adams

Holly Jones pulled her boyfriend to a halt by St Januarius's church wall. She cocked her head over at the graveyard and smiled.

"Been ages since we did it in there!"

Ashley kicked open the battered wooden gate and tugged Holly after him, their laughter echoing off Winfield's ancient walls.

The church bell tolled midnight and the trees leered at them out of the October gloom, their branches creaking. Clouds drifted across the moon, plunging the couple into darkness.

Holly shivered but Ashley clicked on his torch and led her over to the far corner of the graveyard out of sight of the road. Her thrill at the intimacy to come mingled with her excitement at escaping their habitual locations: his car, her flat, his parents' house had all become rather mundane recently.

Ashley pointed to the gnarled hawthorn tree by the back wall, but Holly shook her head. Its bark would be rough against her skin. It was all twisted and bent like a dirty old man, hunched over, watching them.

Ashley giggled.

"Makes you wonder what old pervert lies buried underneath. The hoary bush planted on his grave is so weird! Just look at it!"

Holly pinched him.

"One day they'll bury *you* here, Ash. Randy teenagers will come and shag up against the tree nourished by your corpse!"

"Can think of worse places, provided we're together, babe. Peaceful here. Quiet and restful."

Holly stood on her tiptoes to kiss him. She wanted Ashley, but the fallen headstones were rough with lichen and too chilly to be comfortable to lie down upon. Some of the tombs were smoother but still cold against her back. And the poison ivy curled over some of their slabs had given her a rash last time.

The yew skulked up against the church wall like a brooding old woman. The one time they'd had sex up against it, the thing had left her with scratches from its leaves all up her legs.

Ashley pulled Holly into his arms.

"Come home! Do it there instead?"

Ashley's folks had gone away overnight to visit friends. It was all so middle-aged and staid. Holly shook her head. One day, they'd be as boring as her parents and his. Sometimes it felt like the monotony was already closing over them, holding them in its clammy embrace until they suffocated from tedium. But they wouldn't give in easily.

Holly led Ashley over to the elderberry tree in the middle of the graveyard. Fifty years ago, a bird must have dropped an elderberry while flying overhead and the berry had fallen into the soil of a freshly filled-in grave and taken root.

She peered at the headstone beside it.

JANICE LYNN, WIFE AND MOTHER.

A child's name appeared beneath the mother's with the same date of death. They had been interred together. The elderberry tree that had grown on top of the double grave was verdant and full of life in season. But now the stench of a rotting, damp pile of red and yellow leaves turning to sludgy brown repelled Holly.

Ashley guided her over to the pine tree. It towered behind the church, tucked away from the road.

Holly pulled up her miniskirt and let Ashley enter her. The pine was old, but the bark was still soft and sappy. He settled into an easy rhythm and she half closed her eyes in pleasure.

Out of the corner of her eye, Holly spotted a scurrying shape emerge from the pile of wet leaves. It was a squirrel, but black rather than red or grey. She persuaded herself it was just the odd light from the moon sailing out from behind the clouds playing tricks on her. The squirrel had something in its mouth. Its eyes glowed red, then turned black again. She squirmed and tried to warn Ashley that something wasn't right, but the only sound to escape from her lips was a feeble protest, curling over on itself and wafting away on the night air without ever quite being born.

Ashley grunted in pleasure and Holly closed her eyes, stroking his soft hair and murmuring encouragement. He was almost there, and she loved him so much that when he was satisfied, she would soon follow.

One of the pine's branches creaked overhead. Holly cried out a warning that it might break. Ashley tried to pull her away, but her pullover jumper was now stuck to the tree trunk sap. When he yanked at her clothes to free her, he became stuck too.

The branch cracked, the sound echoing off the pine and around the graveyard. Holly screamed and frantically tugged at her arm over and over, but the more she struggled the more stuck she became. Sticky sap oozed from the trunk, covering her face and dripping down her hair. It tasted foul.

Another branch hurtled past them, crashing to the ground at their feet. Ashley shouted for help, but his cries only bounced off the church walls and around the village. A great yawning sound of splitting wood emanated from deep inside the tree.

The pine opened itself up as if it had been split right down the middle with an axe. It wrapped itself around Ashley, despite his struggles, reforming a perfect surface of bark that left no sign of his abduction.

Holly struggled until her cheek became stuck to its scratchy bark. Sap was the blood of the tree, and she was drenched in it. She sensed that Ashley was already giving up the struggle out of pure exhaustion.

Holly wrenched herself free, but the tree had closed over Ashley with no way to free him. She flung herself back into its embrace and it drew her inside too.

Ashley's fingers intertwined with Holly's and she relaxed, giving herself up to being there with him forever.

The breeze wafted through the graveyard and the pine tree's branches rustled gently with it. Night quietly clouded over Winfield village once again.

John C Adams is a Contributing Editor for the Aeon Award and Albedo One Magazine, and a Reviewer with Schlock! Webzine. You can read John's short fiction in anthologies from Horrified Press, Lycan Valley Press and many others. A non-binary gendered writer, John has also had fiction published in The Horror Zine, Devolution Z magazine and many other smaller magazines. John's fantasy novel Aspatria is available on Kindle. John's futuristic horror novel 'Souls for the Master' is also available on Kindle. John lives in rural Northumberland, UK, and is a non-practicing solicitor.

Ghost hunting in a cemetery is not for the weak spirited.

Amateurs

John Grover

Liza stopped and leaned against a withering tree. "Mikey, slow down," she called, nearly out of breath. "We'll never see the Gray Lady if we rush through the entire graveyard."

"We don't have all night." Mikey stopped, his heart racing with excitement, and waited for her to catch up. He carried his audio recorder in one hand and a PK meter in the other. Liza was expected to be the cameraperson, using her phone to capture any activity on video. "We got a lot of ground to cover and she doesn't appear for that long. You know that."

His younger sister rolled her eyes before dragging herself over to his side. "Okay, okay. We need to pick someplace."

"The mausoleum," Mikey said, pointing into the dusk and the huge stone structure in the distance.

The two teens rushed across the oldest graveyard in town. In fact, it was the oldest one of all the surrounding towns and the only one that was known to be haunted. Its gravestones were ancient; many of them were blackened with age, their writings blotted by the passage of time.

Ornate lawn crypts sheltering caskets beneath them and mausoleums dotted the landscape. Up on a lonely hill sat the remains of an old church whose only congregation these days were the ravens that sat vigilant on its decayed steeple.

Stories of the Gray Lady had circulated in town since before Mikey was born. He loved hearing his grandpa and his friends tell them down at the VFW. He'd never seen her personally, not like some of the old townies had, but he always knew that someday he would. He felt tonight was the night. He hoped Liza did too. He didn't need any doubters cramping his style. If she wanted to be a serious ghost hunter like him, she had to believe. Sometimes he questioned her commitment. He hoped it wasn't a mistake letting her join him, especially tonight.

As the sliver of sun melted behind the graveyard's skeletal trees, Mikey and Liza chose their perch beside the mausoleum. It was said the Gray Lady would sometimes walk in and out of the mausoleums and crypts as if searching for something.

"Testing . . . one . . . two . . . ," Mikey spoke breathlessly into his audio recorder and played it back to make sure it was working. "Good. Are you ready?" He turned to Liza.

"Yes."

"Liza, did you check the phone's camera?"

"It's working."

"I didn't see you check it."

"For God's sakes, Mikey. Here we go. Look, it's fine."

"I just want you to take this seriously. You asked to team up with me."

"I thought it would be fun, but we've come out here two nights in a row and got nothing. We're the only ghost hunters I know of that haven't ever recorded a thing."

"It's gonna happen tonight. I can feel it."

"Sure. If you say so."

"I do."

They hunkered down and waited, letting the darkness settle over the graveyard like a shroud. A ribbon of moonlight cut across the sea of tombstones causing them to glow with a strange, eerie luminance.

Mikey's heart started to beat a little faster and excitement swelled in the pit of his stomach. A chill kissed the air and the night grew late.

After a few hours, Liza checked the time on her phone. "Do we have to stay out here all night again?"

"If that's what it takes," he said through gritted teeth. He knew his tone was obviously annoyed.

She rolled her eyes again as she leaned up against the mausoleum. Mikey tried to ignore her but was convinced this was the last time he would let her tag along. He turned on his PK meter and moved it from left to right out in front of him.

A new thought occurred to him and he walked around the front of the mausoleum and scanned its doors with the PK meter. Liza followed him.

"What are you doing?" she asked.

"Checking the whole thing . . . she might have left some sort of residue or something if she came in or out of here. You never know."

"Okay . . ."

Mikey shook his head and moved on, circling the mausoleum back to the front. He walked up two stone steps to the double wooden doors and brushed his PK meter right in front of them. The instrument beeped for a fading second.

"I think I got a spike!"

"What?" Liza joined his side.

Adrenalin rushed through him. He moved closer to the weathered doors and tapped his foot against them. They creaked open. Mikey froze. He looked at Liza.

"They're unlocked," he said with some disbelief.

Liza's eyes widened.

Mikey reached for them with a hesitant hand and pushed them the rest of the way.

"Wait, no." Liza grabbed his arm.

"What?"

"You're not going in are you?"

"Of course I am. It's an invitation."

"Are you kidding me? This is someone's final resting placing. It's disrespectful and . . . weird."

"This is what we came for. You do what you want but I'm going in." Mikey stowed his PK meter, yanked a flashlight out of his pocket and turning it on, slipping inside.

He heard Liza sigh behind him. "Damn it."

The interior of the chamber was mostly plain. An aboveground sarcophagus sat in the center of it. A small stone table rested at the head of the sarcophagus with a vase atop it. The flowers inside of the vase had long decayed; stems slithering down the side of it like the husks of earthworms. On either side of the sarcophagus within the walls were two smaller tombs. The writing etched into the stone was unreadable from his vantage point.

At the back of the chamber was a stained-glass window. Mikey saw the moonlight glowing behind the glass. He looked around again and moved deeper inside, flashing his light over the tomb. Something caught his attention and he stopped.

"The sarcophagus . . . it's been broken open. Are you getting this?"

"What?"

"You are filming aren't you?"

"I—I . . ."

"Liza," he raised his voice. "Get over here. We need to capture this."

"I can't . . . I can't look inside."

"Get over here!"

Liza edged slowly over. She held her phone out in front of her, trying to reach to where she could record the coffin inside.

"I'm gonna look into it, get the phone over here."

"Mikey please . . . I don't want to see it."

"You've got to get closer. Just look away but put the phone over it."

Mikey pushed some of the stone debris off of the sarcophagus and pushed its cover open wider. It was extremely heavy. He flashed his light inside and his stomach dropped.

"Oh my God. The body . . . it's been . . . been partially . . . eat—"

Liza grabbed his arm hard and yanked his jacket. He jumped and turned to yell at her.

"Mikey look!" Liza said with a loud whisper. "Look!"

He turned to the tomb's door and just barely caught the sweep of a gray cloak through the air with his flashlight.

"There she is!" Mikey almost exploded with excitement.

Outside, he saw a gray-cloaked figure with a hood scurry off through the graveyard. His heart felt like it was going to burst out of his chest.

"C'mon!" He dashed out of the mausoleum.

"Mikey wait."

"We gotta follow her. Hurry! Keep up!"

Liza was a few feet behind him, but he kept on running, the gray figure still in his sights. He chased her toward a lawn crypt and hoped to God that Liza was recording all of this. He looked over his shoulder to see that his sister's face had gone pale white; she looked like a ghost as well.

The Gray Lady curled around the rear of the lawn crypt and temporarily escaped Mikey's sight. He ran as fast as he could and around the back of the crypt and . . . lost her. She was gone.

"Damn it!"

Liza finally joined his side, panting like crazy. "Mikey . . . I . . . can't . . . ."

"Did you get her? Did you get any of her on video?"

Liza nodded. "Yeah . . . I think so . . . .

"That was awesome." He stowed his flashlight for a moment and pulled out his PK meter again. It didn't seem to pick anything up. He spoke into his audio recorder. It had been running the entire time.

"We just had an encounter with the Gray Lady. She

is real . . . . She is **very** real. We may even have video of her. We just got our first evidence ever on a ghost hunt. Finally, after all this time."

He turned to Liza and for the first time, she seemed as excited as he was. "Can you believe it?"

She shook her head and cracked a smile. "That was amazing . . . . I'm shaking all over."

"Me too. I wonder where she faded off to? I wonder if she went inside another mausoleum." He backed himself up to get a good look at the lawn crypt in front of him. He reached for his PK meter. "Can you get the entire crypt with your phone . . ." He backed up a little more, trampling a grave beneath his feet.

"Mikey, be careful. You're on top of a—"

Before Liza could finish, Mikey's leg sunk into the ground and he toppled over with a scream.

"Mikey!" Liza rushed to the ground and grabbed her brother's hand.

"What the hell . . . there's a hole down here. There's no coffin!"

"Get out of there," she pulled as he climbed out of the hole.

Mikey instantly rolled onto his belly and started to dig, scooping piles of dirt and grass out of the grave.

"What are you doing? Are you crazy?"

"I have to see what's down there. It's not a grave . . . at least not anymore." He paused for a second and swung his flashlight's beam on the old stone. "Alistair Bancroft isn't there anymore. He won't mind, right Al?"

"You're crazy if you think I'm going in there." Liza sounded pretty adamant.

He looked up at her and tried to put on his most pathetic face. It always worked when they were little. "C'mon Liza, please? We're onto something. This could be big. We could be the first to unearth some sort of scandal or something. Please . . .?"

She stood with her arms folded, staring at him. She refused to answer him.

"I'm going down there." He flashed his light into the hole, it led deeper underground and he was pretty sure they could squeeze through it.

"This is such a bad idea."

Mikey smiled at her. "I knew you wouldn't let me down. We've been on too many adventures together. You and me against the world, Liza."

"Whatever. Let's just get this over with."

He climbed in first, using his flashlight to guide him underground. In the light he noticed the walls around him were marred with what looked like claw marks. Roots snagged his hair and jacket as he crawled, and he heard Liza mumbling behind him. Her voice sounded hollow and he couldn't make out her words.

Finally, he dropped into a subterranean chamber. He was amazed that it even existed. The tree roots held the walls together. The air was musty, and dust fluttered in his flashlight's beam.

He turned to watch Liza wiggle her way into the chamber behind him and stand up. Her head almost touched the top of it but not quite. Mikey had to crouch a little. She pulled her phone out in front of him and showed him that she was still recording but switched on her phone's light, helping Mikey illuminate the area.

"What is this place?" she asked.

Mikey shook his head in awe. "I have no idea." He whirled the light around and shifted it to the ground. He spotted animal tracks there . . . looked like something with clawed feet. The tracks led off into the dark.

"This way," he said to Liza and started off down the tunnel as it twisted away from him and to the left.

"Mikey, slow down. We have no idea where this goes."

"That's why we need to check it out."

He brushed off her concerns and slowly made his way around the tunnel, following his light, checking out the ground and the walls until he came to a couple of bones.

Mikey stopped and held his hand up to Liza. "Wait a second." He bent to the ground and picked up one of the bones. Liza flashed her phone light across the bone as well. "This bone . . . it . . . looks like it has teeth marks in it."

"Mikey, we should get out of here . . . . I—"

"Hold on. Get this on video." Mikey stopped and looked around. The air was choked with the scent of rot. "What's that smell?"

Liza shivered and swallowed some air.

"Death," a voice grated.

The two of them turned slowly, lights gliding across the ground to pick up the gray figure standing behind them.

The Gray Lady blocked the way they'd come.

"Mikey. . ." Liza whispered.

He stood up slowly, his gaze sweeping over the tattered, gray cloak. "Hello?"

The figure remained silent and unmoving.

"W—we don't mean to disturb you," Mikey continued, his voice stuttering and his hands trembling. "We are just admirers and we—"

"Hello." The Gray Lady rasped, her voice somewhere between nails on a chalkboard and shattering glass.

Liza jumped when the Gray Lady spoke, and she moved slowly behind her brother.

Mikey grinned and stared at her intently. The hood of her cloak hid her face, but he could see an outline beneath it. The folds of her cloak clung to some sort of frame.

"You're not a ghost, are you?" He asked.

Silence answered him for the longest time before the Gray Lady shook her head. "No. Not . . . a ghost. Older than any ghost, but flesh and bone am I." She reached up and slid the hood off her face revealing a pointed bald head and a sunken face, taut with sickly gray flesh. Her pale lips smiled to reveal a mouth full of razor-sharp teeth. The entire cloak dropped to the ground.

Mikey swung his arm around and pushed his sister away. "Liza, run!"

She let out a scream but heeded his cry and bolted down the tunnel. Mikey backed away and started into a run when he saw the creature crouch and leap, hitting the tunnel wall and scaling alongside it with long spindly arms and legs. He screamed too.

He ran as fast as he could, his light dancing all over the walls. Behind him he could hear the thing scraping along the walls, dirt raining into the chamber. Mikey spotted his sister ahead of him.

"Run Liza! Keep running! Don't stop!"

"Mikey!"

Crypt Gnats

"Keeping running for God's sake!"

The tunnel kept going and going. It seemed endless. Mikey's legs were about to give out. Sweat poured down his face but knew he had to keep going. He felt the rancid breath of the creature on the back of his neck, and its stench made him nauseous to the point of nearly passing out. He heard the mad cackle behind him.

Up ahead of Liza, he saw another opening in the top of the tunnel, probably from another empty grave.

"Crawl up the hole, Liza!" He screamed to her.

"Mikey! Oh God, Mikey!"

"Go! Crawl up as fast as you can . . . *Go!*"

He watched his sister force herself up the exit. A sense of relief filled him despite the click of teeth behind him. He knew the thing could easily go up and go after his sister.

When he reached the opening, Mikey climbed up into the bottom of it. Wriggling part way up he stopped, blocking the entrance with his body. He peered up at the top and caught Liza's face with his light. "Go Liza, run! Run as fast as you can . . . . I love you."

"Mikey No! Get out of there. Give me your hand!" She reached her hand back into the hole.

He shook his head. "Go! Go now!"

He turned back to see the creature hanging onto the tunnel's ceiling, grinning at him with rows of sharp teeth. It stared him down with eyes as black as coal and advanced on him.

Liza's screams echoed in Mikey's ears as the thing started to feed. It was the last thing he heard as they merged with his own.

John Grover is a fiction author residing in Massachusetts. He completed a creative writing course at Boston's Fisher College and is a member of the New England Horror Writers Association. Some of his more recent credits include stories in Crimson Streets, Underbelly Ezine, and The Ancient Ones II Anthology, He is the author the new fantasy series Song of the Ancestors and of several collections, including the short story collection Creatures and Crypts for Amazon Kindle as well as various chapbooks, anthologies, and more. Please visit his website www.shadowtales.com or his facebook page

Grave markers that pop up like mushrooms over night
should be viewed with suspicion and caution.

Worn Wood

Kyle Bolan

The cemetery had appeared overnight. Right there in Harry's backyard. All the small, unmarked crosses and gravestones that looked very old and very worn.

Harry dropped his morning cup of coffee the moment he looked out the window and saw it. He absolutely hated cemeteries, hated funerals in cemeteries, hated visiting the deceased in cemeteries, and most of all hated the thought of ending up in a cemetery. He almost spit out the sip he had taken but was able to control himself. He thought of what he should do first, and he decided to call Kate on the phone.

"Is this a joke? Where did they come from?" Kate asked when she drove up.

"So you can see it too? I thought I was going crazy," Harry said and let out a sigh of relief, "I have no idea where the cemetery came from. I woke up, looked out the window, and there it was."

"What should we do?"

"I'm not sure if we should pull 'em out or just leave 'em there," Harry said.

"Don't leave it. That would be weird. Just pull the grave markers out."

"Well what if that disturbs some ancient ghosts that were originally buried here? What if these stones and crosses were generated by some ancient Native American ghosts that are at unrest here on my property?"

Kate walked over and put her hand firmly on one of the crosses that was made of old worn wood. "These are solid. So, not generated by ghostly powers."

"I guess we should just pull them out then," Harry said, agreeing with Kate.

"It was probably some neighborhood kids playing a joke on you. Like crop circles," Kate chuckled.

"Hey. Those are real. They are *not* some kids playing a prank."

"Okay. Okay. Let's start pulling them out. I can't believe you reacted the way they wanted you to."

"Yeah. I guess I was being pretty silly. Evil ancient spirits about to haunt my house. Sounds stupid now."

Harry went over to the nearest cross, got a firm handhold and pulled up. The marker didn't budge.

"Jeez. They really pounded these in."

He took a deep breath and pulled harder. The cross came loose, and Harry suddenly felt a sharp pain on his shins, like a cat clawing him. Then he noticed that the cross didn't feel like wood anymore; it actually felt scaly.

He looked down and, to his shock, what he pulled out wasn't a grave marker. It was a fairly large, lizard-like creature that was swiping at his legs with its long-taloned fingers. Harry dropped the creature in pain and horror and backed away.

The thing fell on its head and, as soon as it regained its senses, locked eyes with Harry, then crawled with incredible speed toward him. He turned and ran, getting safely inside before the lizard thing could catch up.

Harry looked out the kitchen window facing his backyard and saw that all the other grave markers were now uprooting themselves. They were all buried head-first in the lawn, some just so the very tip of their fat tails were poking out, some buried up to where their back legs and belly were protruding from the ground. Harry realized that these things had positioned themselves so they would appear to be worn wooden crosses or small stone markers. It depended on the color of the creatures. The "lizards" that looked like crosses were light brown in color, and the ones that resembled tombstones were light gray.

They all had black eyes on long stalks and flashed razor teeth when they opened their mouths. Their long, thin bodies were supported by extremely long spindly arms and legs that could retract in towards their bodies. When the creatures' arms were retracted, the leathery, scaly skin of their appendages bunched up so much that their arms thickened to more than five times their normal width. *The reason why,* Harry thought, *they were able to look so much like crosses when they were in the ground.*

"I guess this wasn't a prank, Kate," he yelled, and a new shiver of terror swept over him as he realized Kate was still out there with the deadly creatures. He watched through the window and saw that she was backed into the

215

far left corner of his yard. The lizard things were all creeping towards her now. She had no way out.

Harry cringed and tears streamed down his cheeks as the creatures swept over her in a frenzy. She became a whirl of brown and gray that reminded Harry in some remote detached part of his brain of the Tasmanian Devil.

Blood flew out of the frenzy and Harry looked away. When he worked up the nerve to look back, there was no sign of Kate, except for the blood spray on the fence. There was no sign of the creatures either; they had all disappeared.

He got the sense that these things had done this many times before, that they were very experienced and knew exactly how humans would react.

Harry sank into a chair, trying to get a handle on what had just happened, when he heard scratching at the back door. It sounded very weak. *Luckily they can't get in,* Harry thought even though he was still scared.

Hands shaking, he fumbled in his pocket for his phone. With trembling fingers, he hit the emergency button. The second it took for the phone to start ringing felt like an eternity.

Then the reassuring voice spoke in his ear, "911, what's your emergency?"

"There . . . was a cemetery . . . came alive . . . tell everyone . . . ate my friend Kate . . . come quick . . . please help . . . we've got to warn everyone . . . . "

That was all he could manage in his breathless, shell-shocked state.

He hung up and tried to calm himself down, but he couldn't stop shaking. The police couldn't get there fast enough, if they were even coming at all. *They probably thought I was some half-crazed nut.*

Then, he glanced to the back door and saw five heads poking through the crack at the bottom of it. The creatures were flexible and thin enough to squeeze through the tiny opening. Too late, he realized, there was no escape inside or outside.

At least I won't have to worry about ending up in a real cemetery, Harry thought with a touch of ironic resignation as he watched the creatures advance. *There'll be nothing left to bury.*

———————

Kyle Bolan is a speculative fiction author whose stories have appeared in Enchanted Conversation, The Evening Theatre, and Speculative 66. When he's not writing, he spends his time reading and collecting vinyl. Follow him on Twitter @KyleBolan.

Acknowledgements

Thanks to:

All the authors who worked so hard to make
Crypt Gnats possible;

Rhyss DeCassilene and Michael Hanson for their
help on the first draft;

Tom, who had to put up with Crypt Gnats from
conception to print;

Stephen, our webmaster;

Beverly Haaf, who worked with me on Crypt
Gnats without going insane.

JERSEY PINES INK

Look for upcoming books
from Jersey Pines Ink
https://www.jerseypinesink.com/

JumpRope Chronicles continues

Death Counts the Golden Coins

by Ivy C. Leigh

A novel of supernatural suspense

The Chanting

by Beverly T. Haaf